Souvenir guide

The Lorient submarine base

Contents

Historically, the first concrete submarine base was built in Bruges, in occupied Belgium, for the Imperial German Navy, in 1918. U-Boot-Archiv Coll.

Introduction

From August 1917 to February 1918, a huge concrete construction was built in the centre of the Port of Bruges, in Belgium, occupied by the Imperial German Army. To protect their submarines, the *U-Boote*, from the threat of the British aviation, the Germans built the first submarine base in history. Comprising 8 pens, it efficiently protected them from English air raids for less than a year.

History often repeating itself, during the Second World War, 25 years later, the Germans built five submarine bases on the French Atlantic coast, in Brest, Lorient, Saint-Nazaire, La Pallice and Bordeaux, which

The Château de Kéroman, which gave its name to the peninsula where the main submarine bases were built, was situated on the hills beside the cemetery. It was destroyed during the bombings. LB Coll.

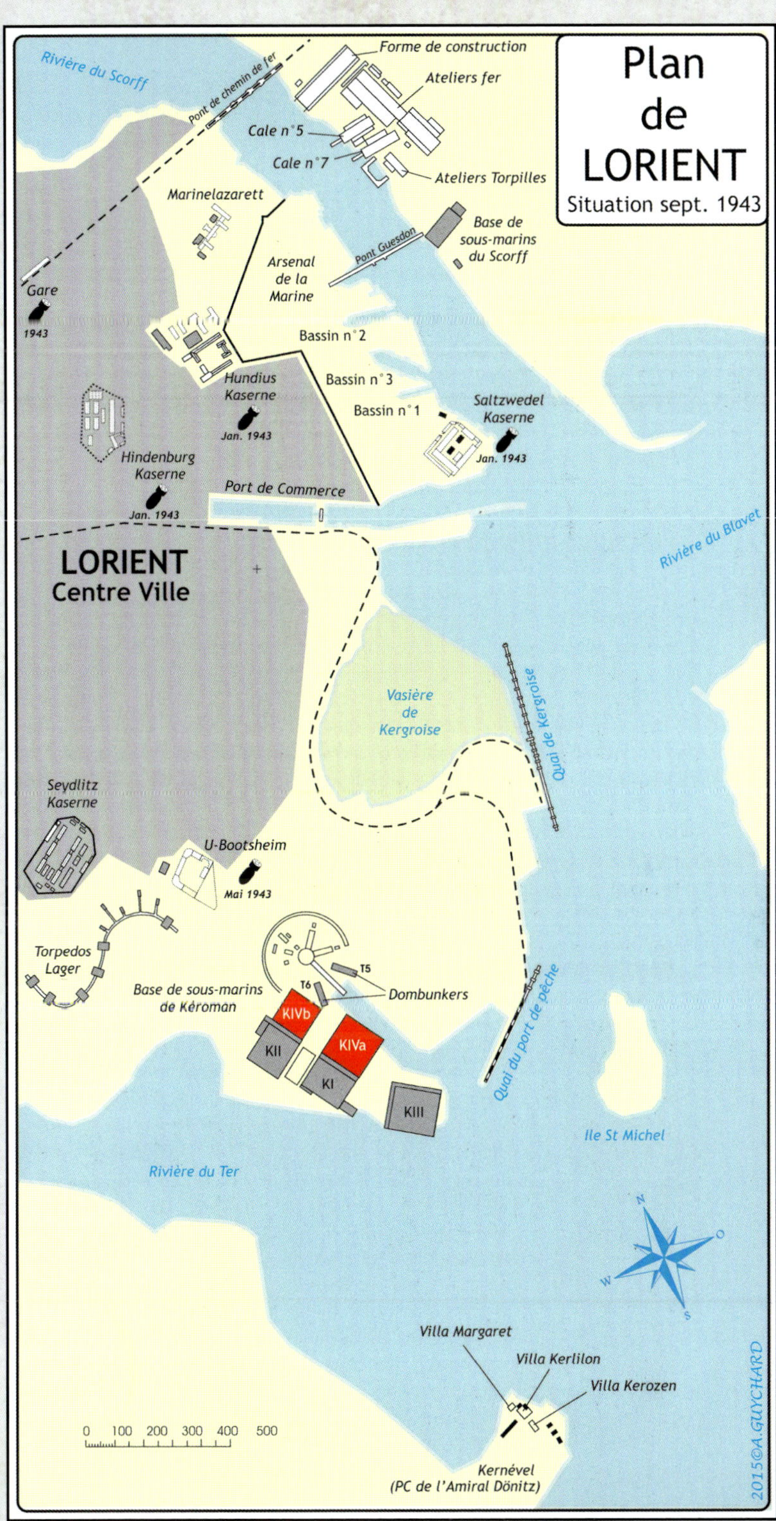

Plan of the German Navy installations in Lorient. Drawing by Anthony Guychard

they occupied from June 1940. In 1943, these 5 German bases on the French Atlantic coast were capable of sheltering 98 German submarines.

Lorient alone could hold 30. From 7 July 1940, which marked the arrival of the U-30 in Lorient, up until 9 September 1944, date at which the last submarine, the U-155, was to leave this base, 203 different *U-Boote* and 2 Japanese submarines were to stop over in this port. Being the main base, during wartime, to be used by the German submarines, it was here that the largest protective construction work for the *U-Boote* was to see daylight.

Discover the deployment and workings of these gigantic buildings in detail in this guide. Learn about the allies' attempts to destroy them and the actions carried out by the arsenal's own French Resistance. Discover the astonishing projects which were never implemented and the role of the bases during the Lorient Pocket. Lastly, this guide will explain how they were reused by the French Navy for fifty years, as well as their current reconversion for peaceful purposes.

October 1940, three German shipyard workers from Lorient passing in front of the old submarine quay crane (left bank, Lanester side), called "station 6" after the war and destroyed in the 1980s in order to build a composite workshop. In the background we can see the railway bridge. The workmen are still wearing the insignia of the Wilhelmshaven shipyard on their forage caps. ECPAD Coll.

A German shipyard created in Lorient

On 10 May 1940, the German forces launched a lightning attack on Western Europe. The French army lost 92,000 soldiers in five weeks. The British, who succeeded in bringing home the majority of the task force they had sent to France, continued to fight alone against the German and Italian axis. The *Wehrmacht* entered the city of Lorient on 21 June, commanded by the Vice Admiral of the Penfentenyo de Kervereguin squadron, commander of the 5th Maritime Region division, after a short battle a few kilometres north of the city. This gallant last stand was made to prevent the Germans from entering the port without a fight, which meant they could consider the French arsenal to be spoils of war. The Admiral had to symbolically hand over the keys of the city to the Germans. However, earlier he had organized the evacuation of all the Navy's ships to sea and had any of the port installations that the occupying forces could have made use of destroyed.

The Franco-German armistice was signed on 22nd June 1940. The very next day, *Admiral* Dönitz, commander-in-chief of the German submarine force, inspected the Atlantic ports and, in particular, Lorient, the tour of which filled him with enthusiasm. Following this visit, on 26 June 1940, the commander-in-chief of the German Navy in Brittany established in Brest, *Konteradmiral* Lothar von Arnauld de la Perrière, the former *U-Boote* record holder in 1914-1918, chose Lorient as the first French port to be used by submarines. Although only part of the arsenal's port installations had been sabotaged, such as the dock gates, their pump installations and cranes, these could be repaired fairly quickly and become key tools. The major strengths of Lorient were the French arsenal workshops, which were immediately operational, and the huge site around the Kéroman fishing port; equipped with modern installations linked by rail, it would make an excellent site for developing a future large base. Finally, the port was safer than Brest, due to its great distance from the British coast. It was also the nearer to Paris for supplies by rail.

As soon as the decision was taken to make Lorient the main operational port for the *U-Boote* in France, a naval supplies department was set up. It was mainly comprised of shipyard workers - *Kriegsmarinewerft* from Wilhelmshaven, the only arsenal that the Germans had kept after the First World War. A party of them arrived on board a special train which Dönitz had organized on 22nd June! Its wagons also contained 24 torpedoes, air compressors and supply equipment. A convoy of trucks loaded with equipment was also sent, under the command of the arsenal's torpedo department manager, *Kapitän-zur-See* Wilhelm von Trotha. During the two first months, the supplies department run by the engineer and *Korvettenkapitän*, Waldemar Seidel, was placed under the orders of the German commander of the port of Lorient. Within scarcely two weeks, these workers were ready to provide any submarine entering the port with a fresh supply of torpedoes, fuel, provisions and water. They were able to carry out repairs from 2 August 1940.

17 October 1940, Vizeadmiral *Hans Stobwasser (left) shows the port of Lorient installations to* Vizeadmiral *Walter Matthiae, who would officially replace him as manager of the shipyard 3 days later.* ECPAD Coll.

Cleared of the danger of magnetic mines by a few of the *2. Räumboots-Flottille* minesweeper launches, the port of Lorient was declared open to the *U-Boote* on 6 July. The very next day, *Kapitänleutnant* Lemp's U-30, which had received the order to go there by cable on 4 July, made it her port of call. For logistics reasons, the submarine bases in France were specialized in the maintenance and repair of one type of *U-Boot* only. Lorient, which welcomed the 2nd Flotilla from July 1940, and then the 10th Flotilla from March 1942, was then destined, as a priority, to receive IX type submarines. However, while waiting for the Brest and St. Nazaire bases to be really operational in mid-1941, the II and VII types were also frequent visitors.

The U-37 was placed in the arsenal's dock No. 2 in mid-August 1940. This dock was repaired by M.A.N. after the acts of sabotage by the French in June 1940. Wolfgang Ockert Coll.

In February 1941, the shipyard carried out work on a IX type submarine and on Prien's U-47 in dock No. 2. Sitting on stocks, the two U-Boote *were superficially camouflaged by nets falling down on either side of the antenna wire. LB Coll.*

Independent as of August 1940, the Lorient supplies department was transformed into the navy arsenal - *Kriegsmarinewerft Lorient*. It then placed under the supervision of an admiral, *Vizeadmiral* Hans Stobwasser. The German workers from M.A.N. were charged with repairing the port installations partially scuttled by the French army, mainly the 3 arsenal docks. The quick work, supervised by *Oberingenieur* Kessel and *Direktor* Breitwiesel, enabled them to place the U-37 in dry dock from mid-August. The only protection against air raids was to conceal the submarine under camouflage nets. The 3 arsenal docks would only be completely operational from mid-1941. Thanks to a metal gate which was added to the centre of dock No. 2, separating this slipway into two distinct sections, the 3 docks could hold up to 8 *U-Boote* at the same time. On 20 October 1940, *Vizeadmiral* Walter Matthiae, was named director of the Lorient *Kriegsmarinewerft* replacing *Admiral* Stobwasser, who left for Brest to carry out the same duties. The 650 German workers who worked there mixed with the French ones, to whom the *Kriegsmarine* had left a small section of the arsenal to work on the warships still being built in the middle of the 1940s, under the supervision of the Engineer, General Antoine.

Merit decoration awarded to deserving officers and workers of the German shipyards in the West. LB Coll.

The workers of the *K.M.W.* were spread out in various workshops called "*Ressorts*": *Ressort I Ausrüstung* - warehouse and supplies had the job of supplying submarines and auxiliary warships with fuel, distributing berths, towing ships to these berths and providing assistance to any ship damaged on arrival. To carry out these tasks, it had 21 tow-boats, 24 patrol boats for the traffic, 6 floating cranes, 39 supply boats and lighters, as well as 350 vehicles (cars, lorries and buses). *Ressort II Artillerie* was comprised of two departments: *II M* armaments charged with servicing guns and handheld arms, *II T* technical workshop for the electrical installations of this armaments store. On the other hand, the supply of ammunition, with the exception of torpedoes, was carried out by the Lorient Arsenal Artillery Department. *Ressort III Schiffbau* - naval architects took care of work to the *U-Boote* hulls, particularly the repair of damage caused by bad weather, allied guns or grenades. This department also removed the seaweed and mussels that might have adhered to the hull during the crossing. *Ressort IV Machinenbau* – machine building was composed of two main departments: *IV U* maintenance of Diesel and electric machinery, *IV E* electric installations. *Ressort V Hafenbau* – port constructions carried out all the port work related to the arsenal, both on shore and at sea. *Ressort VI Navigation* was in charge of fully equipping the naval forces in nautical instruments, charts, ship's log-books, as well as their installation. They therefore provided chronometers, barographs, sextants and spare parts for gyroscopic and magnetic compasses, and repeaters. *Ressort VII Torpedo* looked after maintaining the torpedoes and positioning them in the *U-Boote*. *Ressort VIII Nachrichtenmittelbetrieb* - modes of transmission section was charged with maintaining the radio installations on board the *U-Boote* and all the other floating vessels. This department also established a large telephone exchange for all the departments in Lorient, and also created large radio installations including 16 high-power emitters, enabling the Dönitz staff headquarters to communicate from Kernevel with the *U-Boote* on campaign. The *K.M.W. Lorient* also included administrative, health, staff management, safety and civil defence departments. According to *Vizeadmiral* Matthiae, the *K.M.W. Lorient* workforce, for the Germans, numbered: 33 officers, 115 female staff members, 137 civil servants, 300 male staff members, 4,000 workers and 600 soldiers. For the French, they numbered 4,300 workers and staff, most of which were specialists previously employed by the arsenal. The German workers, who were lodged on site during the first two years of the war, were then moved to camps outside the city, due to the increasing number of allied bombings. The largest of these was the Camp des Genêts, leaving Hennebont on its western side, fitted out with all modern conveniences for 1,400 men.

The standard maintenance and repair process for a submarine would have been as follows: Day 1: the *U-Boot* entered the port and moored alongside a pier, generally on Quai du Péristyle. Day 2: the submarine was emptied. Day 3: the Chief Engineer on board (*Leitender Ingenieur*) and the Chief Machinist (*Obermachinist*) met with the Flotilla's Chief Engineer and the men in charge of the different *Ressorts*.

They presented them with a report on any damage observed during the assignment. A repair schedule was established. Even when the submarine had not suffered any damage during its cruise, check-ups and battery

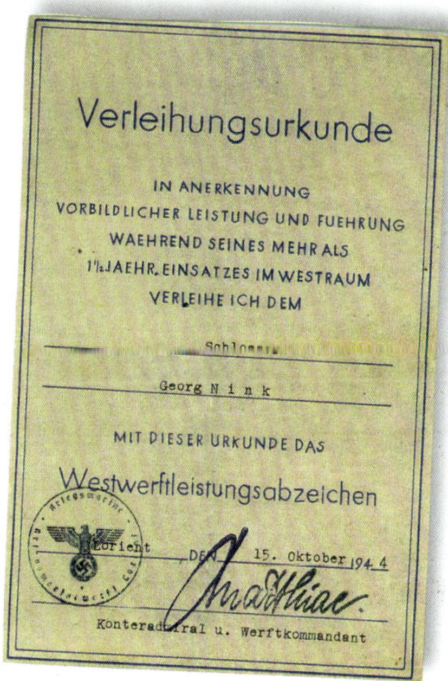

Verleihungsurkunde

IN ANERKENNUNG
VORBILDLICHER LEISTUNG UND FUEHRUNG
WAEHREND SEINES MEHR ALS
1½ JAEHR. EINSATZES IM WESTRAUM
VERLEIHE ICH DEM

Schlosser

Georg N i n k

MIT DIESER URKUNDE DAS

Westwerftleistungsabzeichen

Lorient, DEN 15. Oktober 1944

Matthiae

Konteradmiral u. Werftkommandant

Certificate for decoration awarded to a German ironsmith of the K.M.W. Lorient *signed by the* Konteradmiral *Matthiae, in charge of the shipyard until May 1945. Private Coll.*

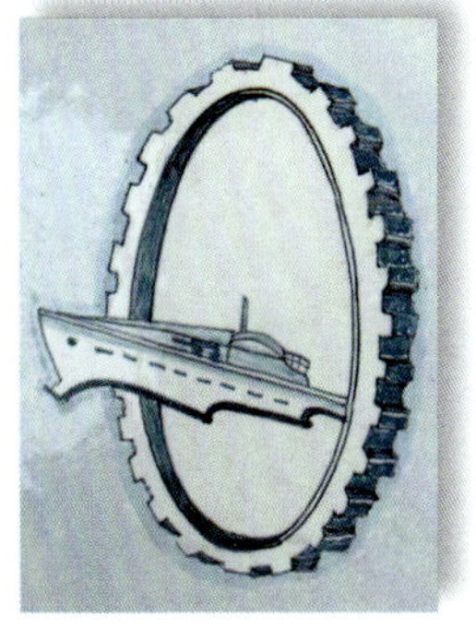

Earthenware tile from Quimper showing the emblem of the shipyard. LB Coll.

On 1 October 1941, the U-124 back from its mission takes a break before entering the Scorff base. Female workers, from German companies, stand on the submarine foredeck to offer flowers to members of the crew. UBA Coll.

repair work lasted at least two weeks. This enabled the crews to rest.

Day 4: the *U-Boot* was taken on by the shipyard.

Day 7: it was put into dry dock for 13 days, to enable work on the hull and reconditioning of the batteries.

Day 20: the submarine was taken out of the dock.

Day 27: general condition of machinery test.

Day 28: the shipyard work was complete.

Day 29: the vessel's crew set off to sea with several specialists from the *K.M.W.* to carry out tests.

Day 30: the torpedo tubes were checked to see if they were in good working order. If the *U-Boot* was declared operational for the front, submarine supplies were loaded as well as food for the crew: torpedoes, *Flak* ammunition, fuel, water, canned food, and fresh food just before setting off. This loading procedure could last for 4 days.

Day 34: departure and deep water diving test. Therefore, the average *U-Boot* repair time was about one month. For this type of maintenance, not requiring any specific work, each submarine mobilized 112 workers, for 23 days of effective work by the shipyard. These can be broken down as follows:

- 40 shipbuilding workers, or 920 working days.
- 45 machinery workers, or 1,065 working days.
- 10 workers specialized in electricity, or 230 working days.
- 17 artillery, torpedo and transmission department workers, or 381 working days.

Before setting off on its mission, to reduce the risk of running into a magnetic mine, the submarine went through a demagnetization station installed in Pen Mané Bay, opposite the old wireless telegraphy station. From June 1943, the *K.M.W. Lorient* was responsible for strengthening the *U-Boote*'s anti-aircraft armaments. With this aim, additional platforms prefabricated in Germany and transported by train were installed behind the submarine conning tower to receive light *Flak* weapons.

Finally, to counter the development of radar equipment on allied airplanes and escort ships, the German Navy had snorkels installed in the bases, to enable the *U-Boote* to sail on Diesel, submerged at periscope depth. This work, which began on 9 January 1944 and was completed on 25 August, equipped a total of 16 submarines in this base.

Kérillon villa, on Kernevel head in Larmor Plage, was requisitioned for Admiral *Dönitz. LB Coll.*

The Organisation Todt *charged with the construction*

On 28 October 1940, *Vizeadmiral* Karl Dönitz, commander of the German submarine force, met Hitler in the vicinity of Paris, when he was returning from his meeting with General Franco in the Basque country. The submarine force commander officially asked Hitler to intervene as quickly as possible with the *Organisation Todt* to protect the *U-Boote* in the 3 French bases of Lorient, Brest and St. Nazaire. On 7 November, the Todt Minister was informed of Hitler's request to build submarine bases in France. This civil engineer, a former aviation lieutenant during the 1914-18 war, had accumulated titles within the 3rd Reich as "general inspector for special constructions of the 4-year plan" and "Reich Minister of armaments and ammunition", was in charge of construction and armaments. At the same time he directed a huge civil engineering organization, which built 3,065 km of motorways in Germany up to 1st March 1939, as well as 13,700 bunkers for the *Siegfried Line*, which stretched for 630 km. This paramilitary organization, which had its own uniforms and specific ranks, would accompany the army everywhere, while remaining independent. Its role was to manage any construction work in Europe of any form of strategical interest: industrial and urban protection, communication channels, hydroelectric constructions, and various fortifications. After the French Campaign, the *Organisation Todt* was charged with the reconstruction of buildings destroyed during battle, deploying heavy batteries in Pas-de-Calais and airfields for the *Luftwaffe*, of which Fritz Todt was *Generalmajor*.

On 11 November 1940, *Admiral* Dönitz officially set up staff headquarters on the Kernevel peninsula in the town of Larmor Plage, just opposite Kéroman, where the three villas, 'Kérillon', 'Margaret' and 'Kerozen' were requisitioned. The first, which was occupied by *Vizeadmiral* Dönitz, was known as 'Sardine Château' by the submariners, because its old owner managed a fish factory. On 15 and 16 November, Todt came to Lorient, to lead the first discussions on submarine shelters with *Vizeadmiral* Lindau, representative of the *Kriegsmarine* High Command in France, *Konteradmiral* Siemens of the Naval Operations Board and *Vizeadmiral* Dönitz.

These two days of work resulted in the definition of a submarine base construction schedule in France, in the ports of Brest, Lorient and St. Nazaire. A total of 35 protected berths were planned for the *U-Boote*; 12 in the first two ports

On March 9, 1941, Minister Fritz Todt, in Luftwaffe *general uniform, came to inspect the Keroman site. LB Coll.*

After the accidental death of Fritz Todt, Minister Albert Speer came to inspect the Kéroman III shipyard, in the presence of the works director and the shipyard director, Vizeadmiral *Matthiae. Coll. HDB Bildarchiv Philipp Holzmann AG*

Nearly 15,000 men were charged with the construction of the Lorient submarine bases for the Organisation Todt *– preparing steel reinforcements between* KI *and* KII. *DR*

and 11 in St. Nazaire. This construction plan was approved by Hitler, during his tour of the heavy batteries of Cap Gris Nez, on 23 December 1940, and implemented the following year. At the same time, the Organisation Todt in the sector of Lorient, the *Oberbauleitung Mitte*, run by *Baurat* Weiss, requisitioned the girls' secondary school to set up its offices.

The German naval engineering board was then charged with giving plans and instructions to the *Organisation Todt* to build the submarine bases. This directly hired a section of the workers and also used large private German building firms to help it build this gigantic construction. It drew up performance-based contracts with these companies and acted as the contractor providing material supplies and construction equipment. Once the contract was signed with the *O.T.*, these large firms were able to subcontract to smaller specialized German or French companies. Any French masonry, joinery, electricity, plumbing, painting company, etc., could thus take an interest in the Todt. For the personnel, this did not change their lifestyle. Those who worked in a French company under contract with the Todt kept the same status and were still paid by their company.

On 8 February 1942, Fritz Todt died in a flying accident. Xaver Dorsch replaced him as chief of the *O.T.-Zentrale*, and Albert Speer in his state duties. Massive recruitment all over Europe brought the Lorient workforce to 12,401 people on 15 April 1942. This personnel was divided up as follows: 5,780 French, 3,178 Germans (2,501 workers, 331 *OT* staff and 346 company staff), 1,296 Belgians, 1,467 Dutch, 501 Spaniards (Republicans having fled Franco's Spain, interned by France), 89 Italians and 90 others with a variety of nationalities.

Working on the construction of the submarine bases in Lorient was to become risky with the greater number of the allied bombings. During British bombings of the night of 16 May 1941, at least 80 workers died in the La Grande Lande and Beg-er-Men camps in Lanester. In the first American bombings on 21 October 1942, most probably surprised by this attack in full daylight, 48 workers were killed when the Crepelle and Le Page workshops, as well as the Camp Siemens barracks close to Kéroman were destroyed.

Finally, on 18 November 1942, 10 others died during the destruction of the workshop of the Belgian Crucifix company. Following these deadly attacks, the workers were moved to ten or so work camps already built to accommodate them. These were safe from bombings, within a 25 km radius of Lorient. Several Resistance actions were aimed mainly at the Organisation Todt equipment depots in the region and even their brothel in Lorient was attacked using explosives on 8 December 1942.

When the Compulsory Work Order (*STO*) came into application on 16 February 1943, the OT used forced labour, with young French people born between 1 January 1920 and 31 December 1924. When the construction work in Lorient was at its peak on 13 June 1943, the Lorient Organisation Todt, then run by Baumeister Hepp, could count on a total of 22,285 workers, nearly two thirds of whom were used for Kéroman. Their total number fell back to 15,301 during the census of 15 February 1944, before dropping totally after the Normandy landings. Up to 2,000 trucks were responsible for bringing all the construction material to Kéroman. Moreover, the *OT* had its own transport department in the West, with *NSKK-Transport-Brigade-Todt*, whose workforce totalled 929 men during the last census.

From 15 June 1944, the German *OT* workers in Lorient began to be evacuated to Germany.

On 4 August, the 5th and last train loaded with men and equipment left. The remaining foreign workers were then dismissed by the chief of naval constructions, *Oberbaurat* Neumann.

Sloping ramps made of wood were built so as to be able to pour liquid concrete into the chutes on the bases' roof. UBA Coll.

The fishing port slipway and Dom-Bunkers

The highly modern slipway of the Kéroman fishing port, inaugurated in 1927, by which six ships could be brought ashore on wooden stocks, was recovered by the German shipyards.

Instead of being used by trawlers, this would be used by submarines. A first type IIC *U-Boot*, the U-59, was hauled up out of the water in the last 10 days of August 1940. Facing the slipway and still in the water, the vessel was brought to lie on a travelling metal cradle to which it was attached. This was then winched up the slope using cables, and laid on a rotating circular platform, which could be positioned opposite one of the six repair locations provided, to which it was then moved.

Wiederſehen war ſeine und unſere Hoffnung.

Zum Andenken
an Herrn
Peter Litzlbauer
Frontarbeiter bei der Organiſation Todt
Hausbeſitzer in Weireth, Pf. Peuerbach
welcher bei Lorient (Frankreich) am 24. Oktober 1942 im 40. Lebensjahre ſein Leben hingeben mußte.

Eltern, Gattin und Geſchwiſter mein,
So gern ſchrieb ich aus der Ferne heim!
Doch heut iſt's zum letztenmal,
Daß ich Euch grüße tauſendmal
Und ſage Dank für jede Gab',
Die ich von Euch empfangen hab'.
Richte an Euch die letzte Bitt':
Vergeßt ja im Gebet mich nicht.
Nur keine Träne, keine Klag',
Der liebe Gott, der mir das Leben gab,
Rief mich ſo früh ins Heldengrab.
Und ich werde in des Himmels Auen,
Im Lorbeerkranz Euch wiederſchauen.

Englmaier, Peuerbach. 4114—42

Notice of the death of a German Organisation Todt *worker, employed in Lorient, as a result of his injuries after the American bombing of 21 October 1942. Coll. LB*

An Organisation Todt *sentry equipped with an old 1914-18 helmet, watching over the construction site in front of* Kéroman III*'s Pens 15-16.* DR

On the front wall of the pen its number and camouflage paint could still be seen in 2008. LB Coll.

On the second fortnight of September 1940, the type IIC U-61 submarine was hauled up onto the fishing port slipway. ECPAD Coll.

However this system was meant for trawlers with a maximum weight of 400 tons and a maximum length of 65 m. Initially it was only capable of bringing type IIC and IID *U-Boote* ashore, since these measured a maximum of 44 m and weighed 250 tons surfaced (empty). The German Navy then strengthened the whole of the traction machinery to be able to haul VIIA and VIIB types weighing 500 tons surfaced.

Their length was 64.5 m for the first and 66.5 m for the second, which was not problematic in relation to the 65 m provided for in the construction of the slipway, even for the VIIB type, since the rear of a submarine rises very quickly above the propeller.

The U-61, superficially camouflaged, was placed on one of the 6 stocks to carry out repair work on the hull. ECPAD Coll.

In February 1941, the work started in the three Breton ports destined to receive the *U-Boote*. The first plans approved in 1940, which anticipated the building of 35 shelters for submarines in the 3 Breton ports, were scaled up the following month, at which time a total of 30 berths were planned for Lorient alone. The work was to become so important that the

Plan of the Dom-Bunker T6 *containing a type II submarine. Drawing by Bernard Paich*

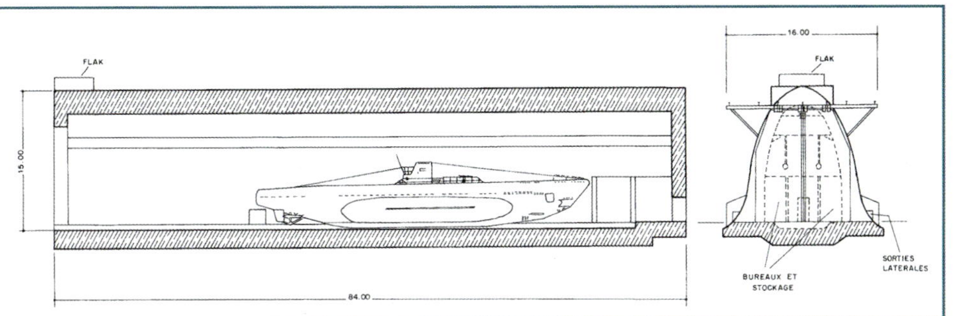

Painting by Ernst Vollbehr dated 2 April 1941, representing Dom-Bunker T6 whose formwork is almost complete. Anthony Guychard Coll.

Spring 1941, view of the bow of a U-Boot *about to be housed in* Dom-Bunker *T6.Two large canvas curtains hide the interior while waiting to receive the protecting armoured doors. DR*

A Type VII U-Boot *sheltered in one of the two* Dom-Bunkers. *NA*

General view of the two Dom-Bunkers, T6 *(left) and* T5, *which were camouflaged by painted zebra strips. They are surrounded by barracks used by the German Navy shipyard. The roofs of the buildings of the city of Lorient can be seen in the background. The anti-aircraft location above the* T6 *was severely damaged during the bombings of 29 January 1943. BA Coll.*

Lorient railway station could no longer cope with the number of equipment trains. A new goods station was set up ten kilometres from there, near Auray. Large sites were then requisitioned for the temporary storage of equipment.

In order to protect the submarines placed on the slipway stocks, which were very vulnerable to aircraft, the construction department requested that the *Organisation Todt* take charge of installing two concrete shelters covering the stocks on which the *U-Boot*'s travelling cradle was positioned. This work was subcontracted to the Carl Brand building firm, from Düren. Two large sheds were built, of a specific shape reminiscent of the nave of a cathedral, called "*Dom-Bunkers*" *T5* and *T6* (the latter with an anti-aircraft defence location), aimed at reducing the effect of bombs. Others were also built in Pas-de-Calais, but here they were used as shelter

View from the rear of the inside of Dom-Bunker T6 *in 2008, with its workshops on either side, and its travelling overhead cranes. LB Coll.*

Plan of the fishing port slipway system sent by Resistance fighters to London. The incline rises out of the wet dock to meet the rotating circular platform. PRO Coll.

During the summer of 1941, just before the Kéroman I *base became operational, the U-79, VII type submarine belonging to the 1st Flotilla, entered the* T6 *shelter. DR.*

for long-range railway guns. This protection work began in February 1941, even though the type IIC *U-Boote*, which were not adapted to the Atlantic, had left Lorient for good, since 3 October 1940. The *Dom-Bunkers*, whose total length was 81 m, were to shelter VIIB (66.5 m) and VIIC (67.10 m) type submarines. Inaugurated in May 1941, and 1.50 m thick, the two *Dom-Bunkers* were the first submarine shelters operational in Lorient. Due to American bombings, which damaged the fishing port slipway on 18 November 1942, as well as other bases being brought into operation and the scarcity of VII type submarines, the *Dom-Bunkers* were sentenced to become mere storage sites for the arsenal.

The small Scorff base

The *Kriegsmarine* construction department also decided to build a small base, for the provision of supplies to 4 submarines, on the western bank of the Scorff, facing the arsenal. From November 1940, the *Organisation Todt* charged the Carl Brand firm with its construction, following the plans provided by the German Navy construction department. The choice of location was essential. The one retained had drawbacks linked to the shallowness of the Scorff and the instability of the ground. The work began with the posi-

General view of the two Dom-Bunkers T5 *(left, housing 3 floors of workshops) and* T6 *in 2008. The uncompleted structures of* Kéroman IV *can be seen in the background. LB Coll.*

tioning of the sheet piles which insulated the construction site from the waters of the Scorff. The muddy soil was then dug out using excavators. However, since water infiltrated, it had to be continually evacuated using a pump system. A total of 2,557 large steel piles, 20 meters high, filled with concrete, were then placed side-by-side to create a stable foundation for the 3 future vertical concrete walls, which were to define the right, centre and left limits of the building, as well as the rear section intended to house the repair workshops. Then came the steel reinforcement of the 3 vertical walls, followed by their formwork using thousands of wooden planks and finally the pouring of liquid concrete. A 3.5 m, A grade protection, reinforced concrete roof, capable of standing up to bombs of 1 ton, covered the top. The progress of the work was too slow and *Dr*. Fritz Todt, who visited the site on 21 April 1941, sent a letter to the Brand company responsible for the work expressing his dissatisfaction. Finally, it was completed on 6 September 1941 by the concreting of a *4 cm Bofors Flak* gun emplacement on the roof.

On 1 October 1941, this small base was officially inaugurated by *Admiral* Dönitz, who welcomed inside the U-124, back from its mission, and congratulated the *Organisation Todt* workers outside. By chance, this base, which required considerable excavation work became operational on the

Period marking, numbering each of the 4 places in the Scorff. Below a stencilled sign indicates that this place is for the movement of staff and tools, and must not be obstructed to allow free passage. LB Coll.

On 1 October 1941, the Scorff base was officially inaugurated. Flags were flown from the front walls of the two pens, each capable of housing two submarines. DR

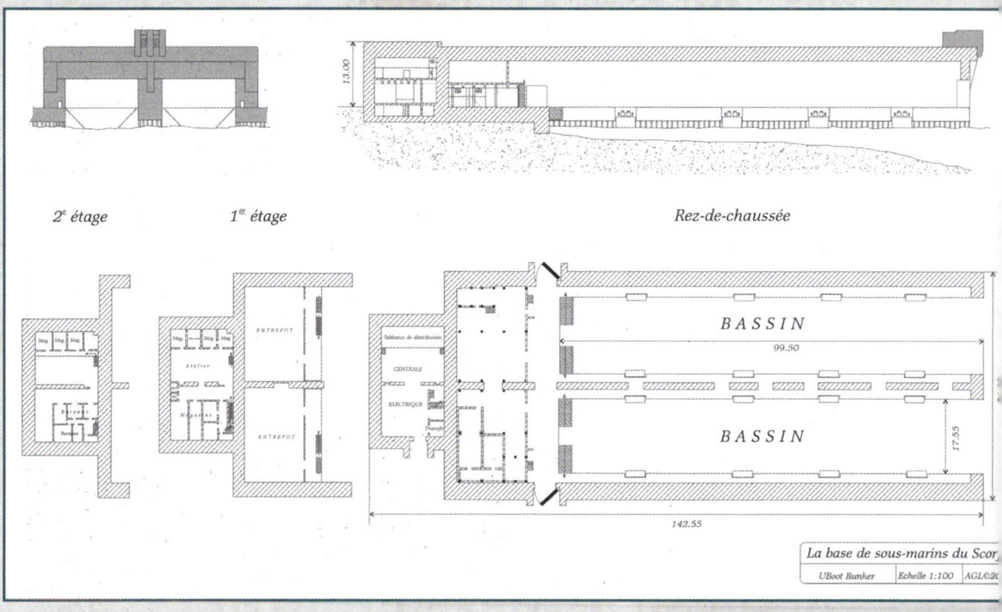

13.00

2e étage   1er étage   Rez-de-chaussée

ENTREPOT

ENTREPOT

Atelier

Tableaux de distribution

CENTRALE

ELECTRIQUE

BASSIN

99.50

BASSIN

17.55

142.55

La base de sous-marins du Scor

UBoot Bunker | Echelle 1:100 | AGL©20

Plan of the small Scorff base and its workshops on 3 floors. By Anthony Guychard

Matching pen in 2008. Coll. LB

A type VII U-Boot *at quay alongside berth 4 in the small Scorff base in 1941.* DR

On 1 October 1941, Dönitz welcomed the U-124 back from its mission inside the left pen of the Scorff base. By his side is the chief of the 2nd Flotilla, Korvettenkapitän *Viktor Schütze. ECPAD Coll.*

The inauguration of the Scorff base, on 1 October 1941, by Vizeadmiral *Dönitz, here thanking the workers, was on the front page of* Der Frontarbeiter, *in August 1942, a German magazine aimed at the* Organisation Todt *workers. LB Coll.*

This technical marking, copied on each of the 4 pen walls of the Scorff base, indicated the place where the U-Boot *conning tower should be positioned. LB Coll.*

same date as the *Kéroman I* structures, which started only 4 months later. The effective width of its two pens being 17.5 m, the Scorff was capable of housing 4 x VIIB/C or IXB/C type *U-Boote*, whose respective beams were 6.2 m and 6.8 m. Located behind the docks were the repair workshops for the shipyard workers.

The small Scorff base, measuring 128.65 m long by 51 m wide, had a specific use. *U-Boote* would pass through them before setting off on their missions. This was where they would be fuelled and receive food supplies for the crew. Moreover, a large fuel bunker was built nearby. The location of this base in a fairly shallow part of the Scorff, however, forced the port commander to have the pens dredged regularly, since they would silt up. In addition, due to the fact it was built on piles, the 3.5 m thick roof could not be reinforced when the Allies started to use more powerful 3,636 kg bombs from November 1942.

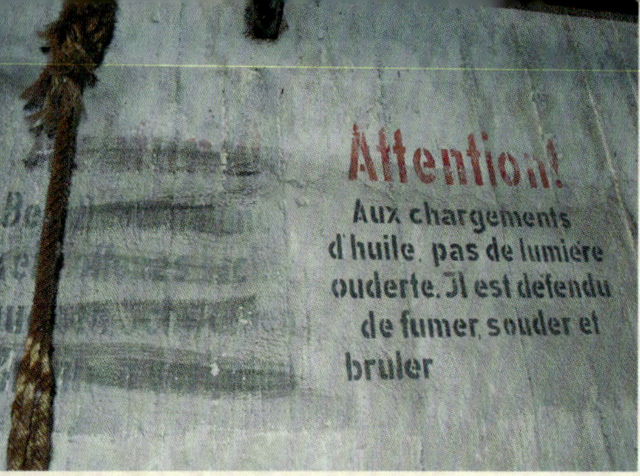

Technical marking in the Scorff. The section in German has been obliterated since the end of the war, while the French section has a spelling mistake in "ouverte"*, probably due to the stencilling being carried out by a German worker. LB Coll.*

Offices for the various technical departments of the K.M.W. *on the 1st and 2nd floors to the rear of the Scorff base, still there in 2008. LB Coll.*

Several members *of the* K.M.W. Lorient *pose aft of a type IX U-Boot, alongside berth 3 in the Scorff base. You can see the workshops in the background, as well as the door leading outside on the left. LB Coll.*

On 1 July 1943, the U-505 left the Scorff base for the Atlantic. It was forced to return to Lorient due to repeated technical problems. Captured by the Americans, this submarine is now on show in Chicago. UBA Coll.

On 11 March 1944, the Kapitän-zur-See, *Hans Rösing, commander of the submarines in the West, came to welcome the Japanese I-29 submarine from the Far East. The submarine was so large that its stern overshot the Scorff bunker! A sign on the workshops in the background says that the space is reserved for the shipbuilding department (Ressort III).* UBA Coll.

The U-546 setting off from the Scorff base for a mission in June 1944. The large fuel storage bunker can be seen to the right in the background. UBA Coll.

Cases discovered in 2008 in a service room of the rear section of the Scorff base: above a case of equipment from the Ressort III *of the* K.M.W. Lorient *(shipbuilders), below a case of 3.7 cm anti-aircraft defence ammunition.* LB Coll.

View of the Scorff base in 2008, with its "Art deco" front behind which was the anti-aircraft defence 4 cm Bofors gun emplacement. LB Coll.

Kéroman I *and* II

Painting by Leo Adler in 1941 showing the installation of the roof on the KI *pens.* Coll. LB

The search for a site on which to build a base capable of housing 12 *U-Boote* began when the Todt Minister left Lorient on 16 of November 1940. The ground was bored at several places and the final location retained was that of the Kéroman peninsula, justified by the fishing harbour, at the mouth of the River Le Ter. Roughly 20 hectares, which were intended for a future industrial area, were delimited and requisitioned on 17 December. The essential factor was the necessity to act as quickly as possible to protect the submarines from British air raids. The choice was made to build the *Kéroman I* and *II* structures, which would not be slowed down by long excavation work. Therefore, these two sites were built above ground. The novelty was in the fact that the submarine was taken out of the water on a slipway system, using the same principle as used at the fishing harbour, to be placed in two bases ashore. With the adoption of this revolutionary system supervised by the naval engineer Triebel, earlier responsible for the same type of work on the island of Heligoland, the only place that needed to be excavated, therefore, was the slipway access, 10.65 m above sea level.

The *Marinebaudirektor*, Triebel, who settled in Lorient in spring 1941, was also the chief of the Technical Committee for the extension of the buildings of all the submarine bases on the Atlantic, until February 1943.

The submarine arriving in the slipway positioned itself above a metal cradle on a wheeled trolley, a watertight lock was closed and the water pumped out to allow the *U-Boot* to sit on the crad-

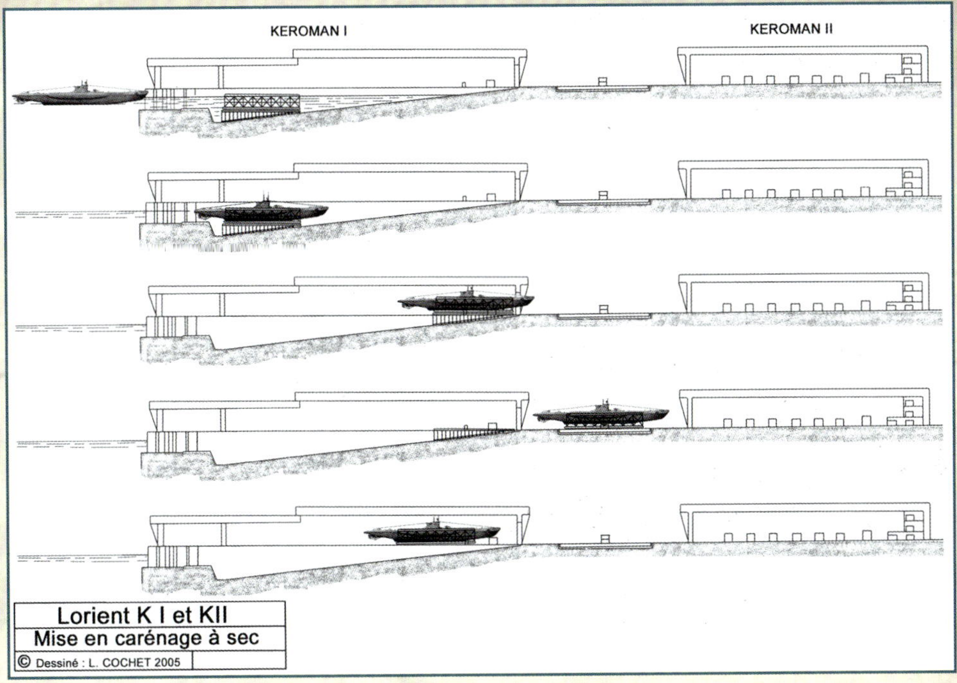

KEROMAN I

KEROMAN II

Lorient K I et KII

Mise en carénage à sec

© Dessiné : L. COCHET 2005

Dry dock plan of a submarine in the Kéroman I *or* II *pens ashore.*
By Laurent Cochet

End of construction for Kéroman II *(left) and* Kéroman I *(right), where a glimpse of the slipway bringing submarines into dry dock can be seen. LB Coll.*

A type IX submarine entering the protected bunker of the slipway. LB Coll.

le. Then together, by means of an electric winch, they were winched up the 10% incline to the exterior, where they stood on a mobile platform.

Driven by an electric engine, this platform moved laterally on 8 rails laid on the esplanade between *KI* and *KII*. Once the submarine was positioned in front of its future pen, it was moved inside, still on its individual travelling cradle, using a tractor. The two large steel doors then closed to protect it. The operation of bringing it into one of the 12 dry pens lasted for a full 46 to 60 minutes, as did the launching procedure when the work was completed. All the elements of

The huge armoured door protecting the rear of the slipway gives us a good idea of the size of the pens. LB Coll.

Painting by Adolf Bock in 1941 showing the entrance to KI*'s slipway. NA*

Once the U-Boot *was in the protected slipway bunker, a watertight lock was closed and the water emptied so that the submarine came to sit on its individual travelling cradle. Together they were winched outside in the direction of a mobile platform. Alain Chazette Coll.*

First dry docking of a U-Boot *in Lorient, in pen No. 1,* Kéroman I, *on 25 August 1941. This was the U-123 commanded by Reinhard Hardegen. In the foreground a lorry used by the* Organisation Todt *workers. MAN Archives Coll.*

The U-123, sitting on its travelling cradle, slides from the mobile platform towards Kéroman I *pen 1. MAN Archives Coll.*

Members of the submarine crew and K.M.W. Lorient *sitting on the stern of the U-123 as it is brought into* Kéroman I *on 25 August 1941. MAN Archives Coll.*

the slipway system, including the rails, the 12 metal cradles on wheeled trolleys for each submarine, the two mobile platforms and the two tractors were prebuilt by the MAN firm from Gustavburg and brought by train.

They were unloaded at Place Jules Ferry, which was converted into a huge storage area in early 1941. The elements making up the cradles were assembled there and then transported by sea, from the floating dock, to Kéroman.

The work started in February 1941. It was carried out by the German firms of Philipp Holzmann from Frankfurt and Siemens Bauunion, united to form a working community through an agreement with the *Organisation Todt*. *Kéroman I* was the first to start. This section, 120 m long by 85 m wide, which included the protected mechanism of the slipway, bringing the submarine under cover, enabled the dry docking of five submarines (pens No. *K1* to *K5*). The pens were covered by a 3.5 m thick roof. The

The U-123, sitting on its travelling cradle, has been brought under cover in the K-1 *pen. It has left the mobile platform still located on the esplanade between the two bases ashore. MAN Coll.*

Page opposite: the maintenance work could begin, particularly on the submarine hull, sheltered from bombs. UBA Coll.

Model representing Kéroman I *and* II *used by the engineers of the German shipbuilders and the* Organisation Todt. *UBA Coll.*

framework of this was made up of an assembly of metal joists made by the Dortmunder-Union company, which was also responsible for their implementation. These were sent directly from Germany by train, already mounted. They were positioned above the pens using cranes and cast into the concrete in the midst of 49 kg per m³ iron reinforcements. The anti-bomb structure, called "*Fangrost*" made of concrete joists, the purpose of which was to make the bombs explode before they reached the next slab, was never installed, but three anti-aircraft defence emplacements were located there. The work for *Kéroman II*, measuring 120 m long by 128 wide, capable of housing 7 *U-Boote* (pen Nos. *K6* to *K12*), did not begin until May. On 25 August 1949, the U-123 was the first submarine to enter *KI*. The official inauguration of the base took place on 1 September 1941, while *Kéroman II* became operational in December. A total of 60,000 small trucks of materials (cement, gravel, sand, rods) were used, as well as 40,000 m³ of timber for formwork!

Not all the submarines could enter these *KI* and *KII* pens ashore; whose effective length was 86.72 m. Such was the case of the type IXD and XB *U-Boote*, which were too long, and the future modern XXI types which were too high! On the other hand, several ships were winched into Kéroman I to be careened, particularly submarine chasers, whose 14th Flotilla was based in Lorient from January 1942.

For the work on the submarine, each pen was equipped with at least one travelling bridge to which a 1 to 3 ton crane was attached. However, this crane was not sturdy enough to carry out the dismantling of a diesel engine, which could be done in one of the arsenal docks. This could be done later when 30-ton cranes were installed in *Kéroman II* pens 23 and 24. In add-ition, since the periscope, requiring regular servicing, could not be

The 7 pens of Kéroman II *in 2008. At the back is the* K6A *pen planned for the storage of the mobile platforms on the ground-floor and to be used as a barracks above. LB Coll.*

The "barracks for the 1,000", where sailors hung their washing on the metal safety rails. LB Coll.

dismantled inside the pens, a one-ton travelling crane especially intended for this manoeuvre was installed on rails along the *KII* roof.

Beside *Kéroman II*, a space the size of a pen called *K6A* was used to store the two mobile platforms, measuring 48 m long by 13 m wide, out of harm's way. Above, a large barracks housed the 1,000 men of the arsenal staff. It was equipped with all the facilities the men needed for living: air-conditioning, heating, dining rooms, changing-rooms and even a cin-ema, with the exception of the toilets and kitchens built in a camp outside, which were destroyed shortly afterwards, during an air raid!

The base defence garrison passes alongside Kéroman II. We can see the "barracks for the 1,000". Michael Schmeelke Coll.

Room in Kéroman I *that kept its original paint and wooden floor until 1999.* LB Coll.

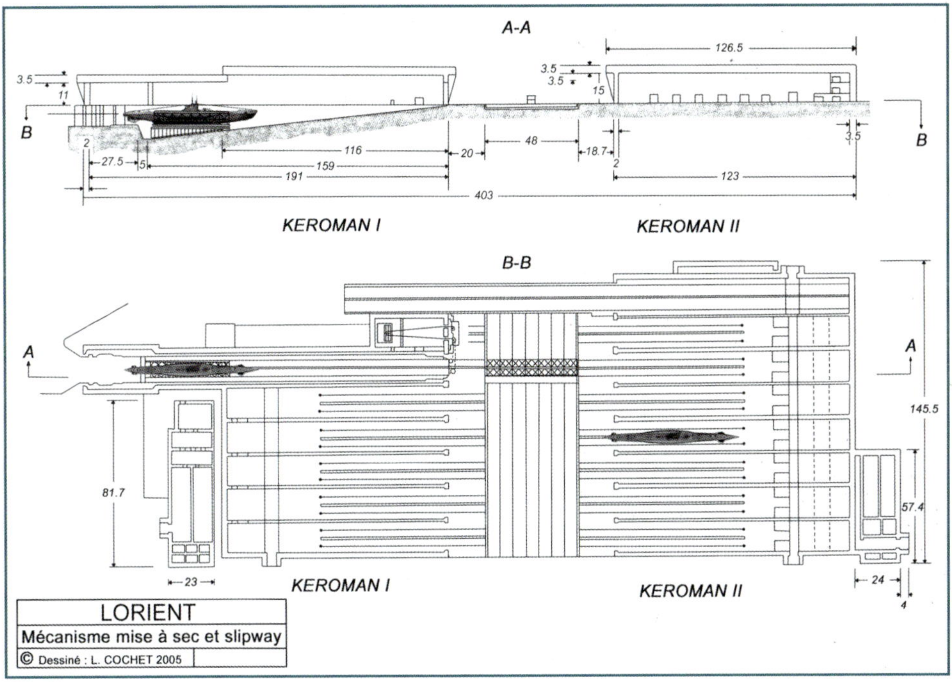

A-A

KEROMAN I

KEROMAN II

B-B

KEROMAN I

KEROMAN II

LORIENT

Mécanisme mise à sec et slipway

© Dessiné : L. COCHET 2005

Plan of the Kéroman I *and* II *bases and their annexes. By Laurent Cochet*

In 1942, the addition of a protected technical area 81.7 m long by 30 m wide was made to the rear of *Kéroman I*. This was to shelter the power generators, heating installations and various oil tanks. Behind *Kéroman II*, another construction, 57.42 m long and 24 m wide sheltered an oil

The power station generators behind Kéroman I *were to convert 6,000 V energy into 380 and 220 V current. ECPAD*

Wall painting by a German navy accordion player on the 1st floor of the rear section of KI. *LB Coll.*

Wall painting of the Englishman "fished up" by a German sailor on the 1st floor of the rear section of KI. *LB Coll.*

Drawing of a combat between several U-Boote *on the way to Lorient and allied aircraft, painted in the* KI *basement. Anthony Guychard Coll.*

The guard carrying out its patrol in front of Kéroman II, *whose pens' protecting doors have been camouflaged! Note the bicycle shelters between the doors. Michael Schmeelke Coll.*

On 16 October 1941, the U-67, whose stern had undergone damage following the attack of the British submarine Clyde, on 28 September at the island of Cape Verde, was brought into Kéroman to shelter. Here Admiral *Dönitz congratulates the* Korvettenkapitän *Schütze, in charge of the 2nd Flotilla. One month and 10 days of work would be needed before it could set off again. ECPAD Coll.*

tank, the 1,350 m³ fresh water tank, as well as transformers, which received high-voltage 60,000 V energy from outside. Here this was converted into 6,000 V and then sent to the power station behind *Kéroman I*, where it was converted into the 220 V or 380 V current supplying the machines and lights in the various bases. A service underground passage linked the three bases, distributing water, oil, compressed air and electricity everywhere. Later, a large energy bunker was also built between *KI* and the future *KIII* base, to prepare for any break in high voltage supply from outside. To the side of *KI*, a training tower was built with a 7 m deep tank, which enabled the submarine crews to simulate the evacuation of their vessel while submerged. Finally, about 800 m north of Kéroman, 6 conc-

On 22 February 1944, the U-530 returned to Lorient safe and sound, from where it would leave only 3 months later. It was severely damaged during an attempt to sink it by a tanker, which attacked on 29 December 1943 in the Caribbean. In the background we can see an empty travelling cradle ready to enter the slipway to recover a new U-Boot. UBA Coll.

Maxim by Bismarck painted in the rear area of Kéroman I *used as an infirmary* "To be German means to be a fighter". *LB Coll.*

Training in the emergency evacuation of a U-Boot *in a tank, as would have taken place in the training tower beside* KI. *LB Coll.*

Wall painting with drakkar and submarine meaning: "Dare to be more audacious, seek to achieve the greatest height, bear the greatest load; a German life" *in the* Jaguar *torpedo house 800 m north of Kéroman, a bunker no longer in existence. Alain Chazette Coll.*

rete shelters were built to shelter the torpedo reserves, to which they were linked by railway.

Kéroman III

The construction of *Kéroman III* was scheduled during the visit of the Todt Minister on 10 March 1941, following the decision by the high command of the German Navy to bring the number of protected berths for *U-Boote* in Lorient to 30. 20 berths were also planned for Brest and St. Nazaire and a

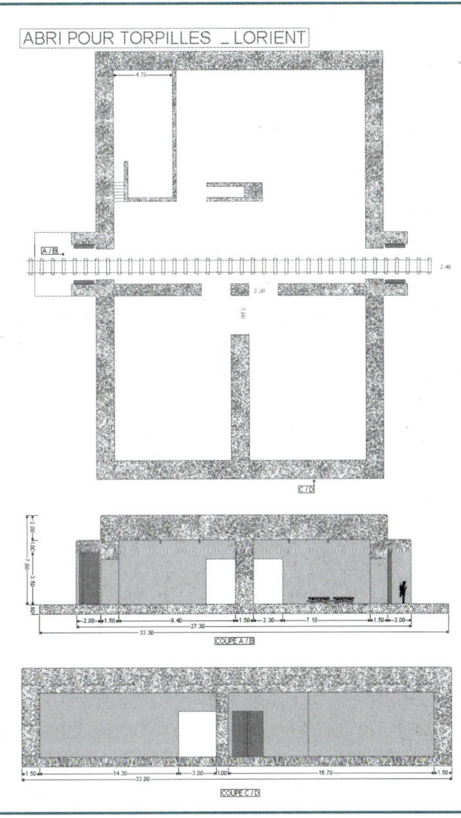

Plan of a small torpedo bunker from the Kerolay position. By Patrick Fleuridas

Large Kerolay torpedo bunker, known as "Iltis". *DR*

base was planned in La Pallice. The work started in October 1941, even though *KII* was not yet operational. Unlike the two previous ones, *KIII* was to be a more traditional base giving directly onto the sea, as is the case of the bases built in Brest and St. Nazaire. To dig the ground, the site had to be insulated using sheet piles. The size of this base was impressive; 168 m long by 142 m wide and a floor area of 24,000 m². It contained 7 pens, which could house a total of 13 *U-Boote* (berths numbered from *K13* to *K24*). To be capable of housing all submarines types, three pens had an effective depth of 98.50 m and two of 95 m, even though the longest *U-Boote* measured 87.6 m (IXD2 types) and 89.8 (XB type).

The sheet pile barrier was dynamited in October 1942, allowing water to flood into the pens. Their lateral walls were already completed. In February 1943, after the pens were roofed and the interior fittings were complete, *Kéroman III* became operational, following fifteen months of work. On 15 November 1942, the U-67 was the first submarine to enter a completed pen in this base. The large workshops situated to the rear of the pens were covered with a 3.60 m thick roof. The roof located above the pens, initially 3.80 m thick reinforced concrete, was strengthened by the addition of 2 extra metres, in July 1943, and then partially with the "*Fangrost*" structure. This brought the protective slab to a thickness of 9.4 m! The colossal roof protection work continued until 11 June 1944, when the workers went on a general strike.

Several German firms were charged with fixing the interior fittings in the pens as soon as their roof structures were completed: travelling bridges, 5-ton cranes in all the pens, and 30-ton cranes in pens 23 and 24 for the dismantling of diesel engines, doors to isolate the pen from the River Le Ter, pumps to empty them of water, machines and tools, etc. Not everything was completed in July 1944, for example only 14 pumps of the 16 intended were installed. Likewise, only pens 23 and 24 were

7 *May 1942*, Gross-admiral *Erich Raeder, Commander-in-Chief of the German Navy, visited the* Kéroman III *construction site. He was accompanied by* Admirals *Dönitz (left in the photo) and Matthiae, the arsenal manager (right). In the background are small trucks loaded with materials to be brought to the construction site. LB Coll.*

Still isolated from the sea by a barricade of sheet piles, this Kéroman III *pen is being roofed with an initial assembly of metal joists. U-Boot-Archiv Coll.*

equipped with fully watertight floating gates, while pens 13-14 and 15-16 had hinged doors, which were never really effective.

Several annexes were built around *KIII*. In mid-1943, the base was made larger by a huge storage space on two floors on the left side, measuring 20.75 m wide by 153 m long, with a 3.50 m thick roof. This was where the 7 freshwater tanks, holding 2,000 m^3, were installed.

Covering its full rear was a space, 14 m wide by 163 m long, covered with a 2 m thick roof, in which there were firing embrasures for machine guns. Then, three successive defensive bunkers were fixed to the groundfloor of *KIII*, for heavy machine guns, while three concrete emplace-

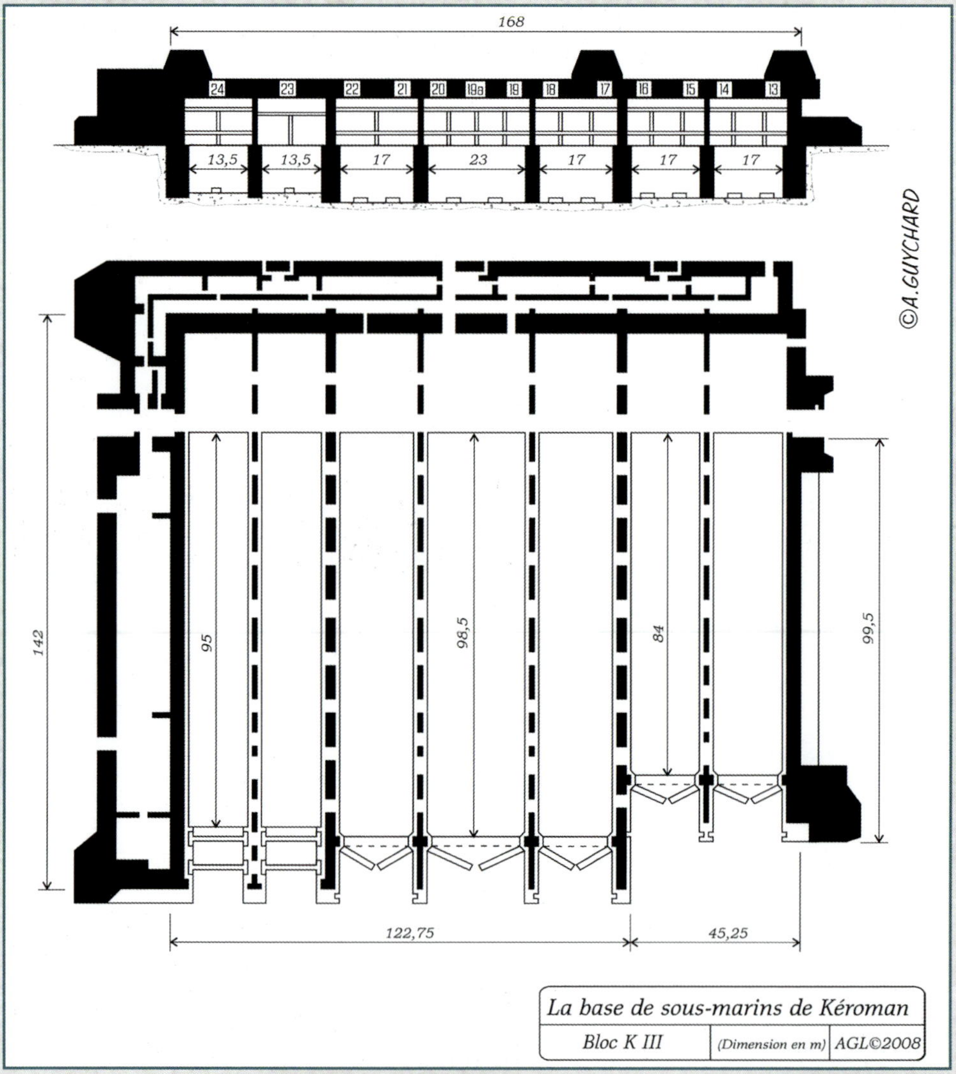

©A.GUYCHARD

La base de sous-marins de Kéroman

Bloc K III | (Dimension en m) | AGL©2008

Plan of Kéroman III.
By Anthony Guychard

The inside of Kéroman III *pen No. 24 in 2008. On the right, the spaces through which you could go into pen 23. The repair workshops and the travelling bridge carrying a crane, with which work was carried out on the submarines, can be seen at the back.* LB Coll.

The Kéroman III *base was completed. On the left, we see the 5 longest pens and on the right the 2 shortest. On the roof the 3 concrete anti-aircraft defence emplacements were built. Left of this base, the entrance to the slipway for* Kéroman I *and* II. *To the far bottom right, the bow of a* U-Boot *about to enter the base. U-Boot-Archiv Coll.*

The roof of KIII *is made up of several levels, the last of which, seen here, is that of the concrete joists of the first part of the* "Fangrost" *structure. Other rounded joists should have been positioned above them perpendicularly, to explode the bombs before they reached the slab below. We can also see two or three anti-aircraft defence emplacements for 2 cm guns. Their tubes were removed after the Liberation. ECPAD Coll.*

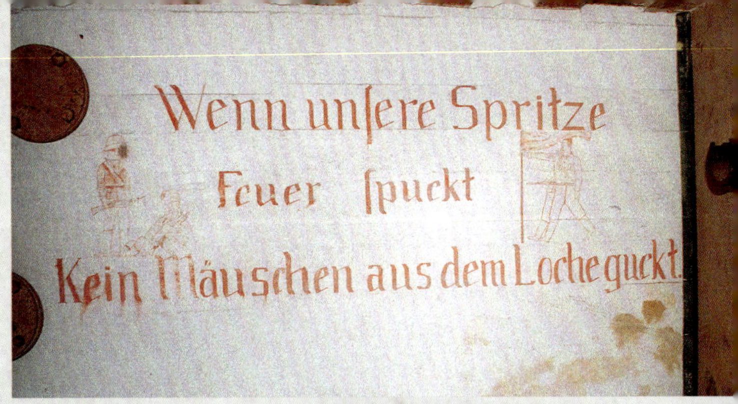

Wall paintings in the combat blockhouse on the fore right-hand corner of KIII. *From top to bottom:* "When we fire continually, not even a mouse looks out of its hole." "Visit to the bunker barber - Do you want your hair back, Sepp? - No, you can keep it!" *The musicians. LB Coll.*

This KIII *pen, with berths for two* U-Boote, *numbered 15 and 16, was equipped with a double metal lock to keep the water out. It could then be dried out using a pump system in order to dry dock the submarines. We can see the travelling bridge equipped with a 5-ton crane. LB Coll.*

This concrete block-house, built on the fore right-hand corner of KIII, *was for a heavy machine gun, whose carriage can still be seen. On the right, a panoramic sight for firing gave distances to the opposite bank.* LB Coll.

On 14 February 1943, the U-105, which had returned from the Caribbean, entered Kéroman III, *with the help of a small tow-boat. The crew lined up on the foredeck to greet the workers waiting for them on the quay running along pen 18.* UBA Coll.

Located between the repair workshops and the pens, a railway enabled trains from outside to unload under cover. The workshops to the left underwent several transformations during the time they were used by the French Navy. LB Coll.

On 4 January 1944, the U-618 arrived in Lorient. On board were 21 survivors of the German destroyer, Z 27. It remained there for one month and a half before attempting to move to the Mediterranean. LB Coll.

ments, each for a *2 cm Flak* gun were built into the roof, with lodgings included for the gunners.

Finally, in 1944, to avoid launching aerial torpedoes inside the pens, the *Strasbourg* cruiser, used as an anti-aircraft defence boat in the harbour, and the *Crapaud* were sunk in front of *KIII*. Large masts were fixed to their structure and linked by metal cables. However, sufficient space was left for the *U-Boote* to manoeuvre and enter the pens.

With the construction of the Kéroman III base, which was operational

On 19 February 1944, the Feldmarschall *Erwin Rommel, inspector of the Atlantic Wall, came to visit the* Kéroman III *installations. He was guided, to the left, by* Konteradmiral *Matthiae, in charge of the shipyard, and, to the right, by* General der Artillerie, *Wilhelm Fahrmbacher, chief of the German army in Brittany and future commander of the Lorient Pocket.* BA *Coll.*

This room, which was accessed from the rightmost pen of KIII, *used in the past to store oil, kept its original equipment until 2007: armoured doors, ventilation and 200 litre drums!* LB *Coll.*

in January 1943, the objective of 30 protected berths for the *U-Boote* in Lorient was achieved: 1 in a *Dom-Bunker*, since the second was converted into a workshop, 4 in the small Scorff base, 12 in *Kéroman I* and *II*, 13 in *Kéroman III*. In comparison, each of the bases of Brest and St. Nazaire could house 20 *U-Boote*; the one in La Pallice, 13, and Bordeaux, 15.

Kéroman III *in 2008. We can still see the camouflaged paint and the number on the front of the pens. LB Coll.*

Resistance to the French arsenal

On 18 June 1940, when General De Gaulle made his celebrated call to the Resistance from London, the Navy forces stationed in Lorient received the order from the French Admiralty to evacuate the port. It was the reverse for the staff working at the arsenal, who, the day after, received the order from Admiral Darlan, commander-in-chief of the French Navy, not to evacuate so that the 4,000 workers' jobs would be maintained. Up to 1944, the German Navy tried everything possible to recover this specialized labour workforce to its advantage. The role of the French managerial staff in this occupied port was the complete opposite. They tried to maintain these workers under their control for as long as possible, so that they would not be used by the occupier. There was little room for leeway. Often concessions would have to be made to save those that could be saved, while waiting for the Liberation and activities to pick up again. The directive from Admiral Darlan on 30 September 1940 stated: "*It would appear to me pointless to seek to stand in the way of German requests. A refusal would have no other result than to lead to restrictive measures together with serious consequences. The only realistic solution is to accept the German requests in principle and seek to obtain as much compensation as possible. Outside their intrinsic advantages, these compensations would enable the government's attitude to be justified among the labour staff of the shipyard and obtain normal activity*"

Drawing of the interior of one of the Dom-Bunkers *in a confidential US report. NA*

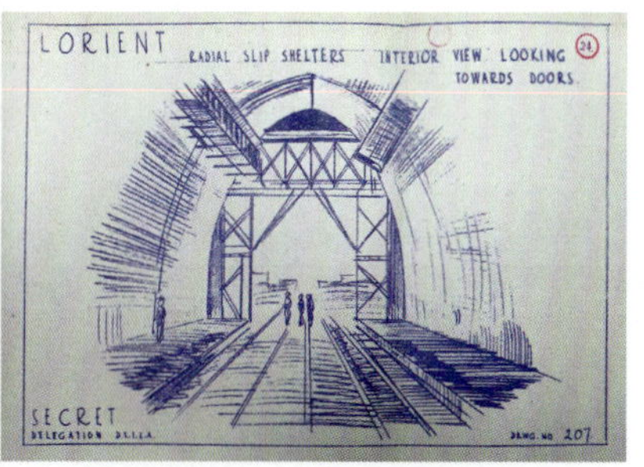

Up to October 1942, the French arsenal managed to hang onto its employees fairly well, by getting them to restore the

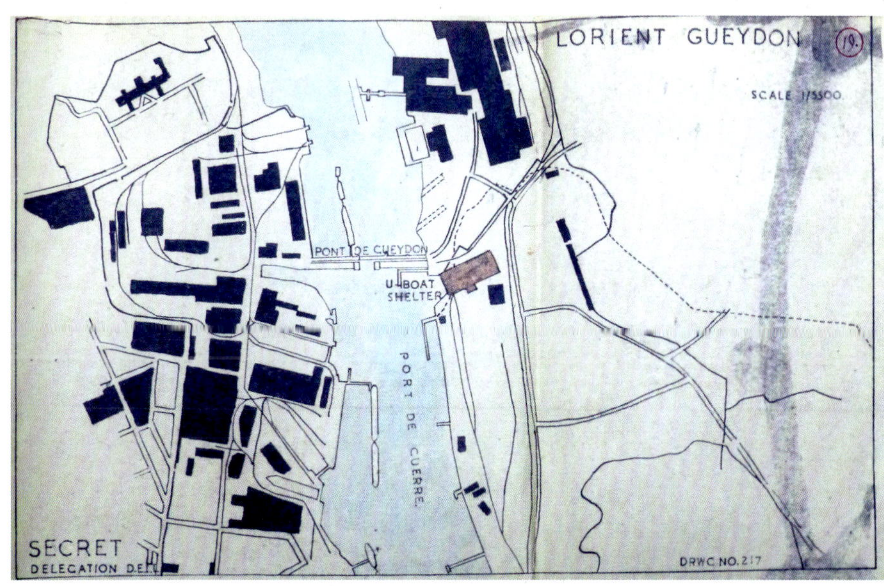

Plan of the location of the Scorff base in the US secret report. NA

Drawing of the base of the Scorff from a photo of the inauguration. NA

The naval weapons building in the French arsenal was used for carrying out maintenance and repairs on the type IX U-Boote *10.5 cm guns. ECPAD Coll.*

installations that were sabotaged in 1940. They also continued to work on three ships, uncompleted in 1940; the 8,948 ton cruiser, *De Grasse*, and the minesweepers A and B.

A section of the workers even worked under French management in the Naval Weapons sectors, which took care of *U-Boote* ammunition as well as warheads and firing pistols. The dispatching of 207 arsenal workers to Germany, in October 1942, did not make relations between managerial staff and workers any easier, as the highly respected

A visit was organized by Admiral *Matthiae, chief of the German shipyards, for two French admirals. Here, they are leaving the artillery equipment workshop, located to the rear of* KI. *UBA Coll.*

Engineer, General Antoine, arsenal manager, was replaced at the same time. With the mas-sive allied air raids, the French arsenal workshops were destroyed one after the other. From 1 March 1943, a large section of the French labourers, working at the arsenal beforehand, were tempted away by the German shipyards, which took care of their supervision using German staff. To guard against any act of sabotage, *Admiral* Kinzel, chief of the German arsenals in France, published a note, on 1 March 1943, requesting that "*French workers employed in the German arsenals may not work in teams, or with their management*". By aligning French salaries with those of German workers and by applying a bonus system, the number of workers in the French arsenal dropped to roughly 1,500 men, while a total of 4,300 French workers and employees were recruited directly by the German Navy. The French workers working at the *K.M.W.* were soon almost as many as the Germans. Finding "*Kriegsmarinewerft*" difficult to pronounce, and in reference to the feldgrau colour of the Ger-

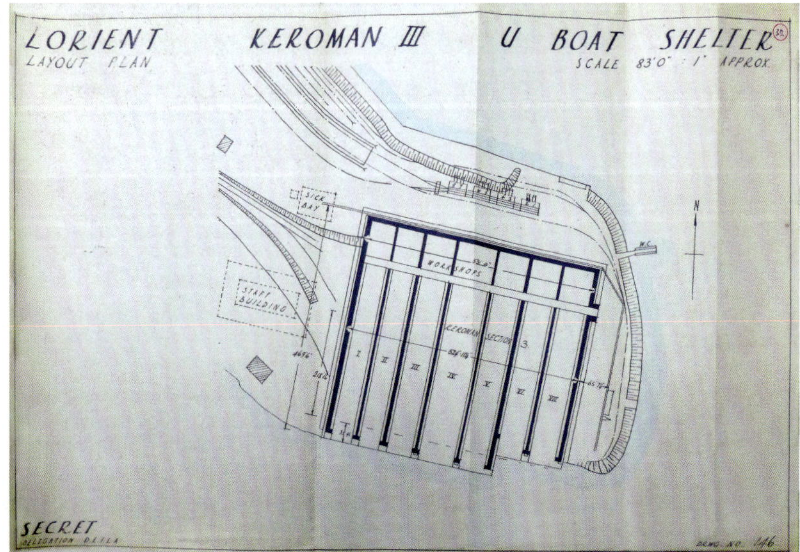

Plan of KIII. NA

Fig. 4.

A. Service passage
B. } C. } Workshops
D. Partition between ground floor workshop and service passage
E. Gallery alongside pen
F. Crane-carrying corbel
G. Guard room (?)
H. Passage
J. Stairways
K. Balcony
L. Ground floor workshops
M. Door
N. Window
P. Doorway

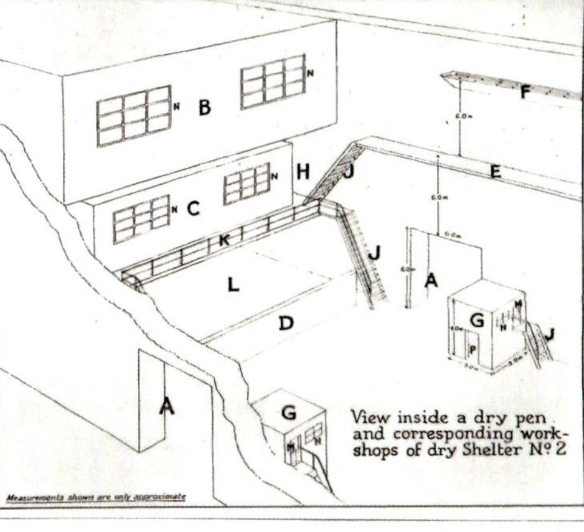

Sketch of a typical interior workshop at the bottom of a KII *pen, based on information provided by the Resistance.* NA

man Navy uniforms ashore, between themselves these French workers said that they worked in the "*marine verte*" (green navy). However, only the German members of the *K.M.W.* were authorized to enter the submarines.

There were a large number of acts of sabotage, mainly in the French arsenal.

From December 1940 to January 1940, at least 18 acts carried out by the Resistance were officially registered. From July 1943, the acts of sabotage were to multiply around the city, involving mainly wires being cut and

AXE

An axe painted in yellow at an angle of 45° on starboard side of c/t. A U-boat bearing this device stopped a lifeboat with survivors from S.S. INGERFIRE on April 12, 1943, 12 hours after INGERFIRE was sunk at pos. 51.29 N.-42.59 W.

Drawn from description.

A 750-ton U-boat with golden axe on C/T arrived Lorient 19 August 1943.

Example of an emblem noted by a Resident on a U-Boot *in Lorient on August 19, 1943. All the identified emblems are grouped together in an American naval intelligence manual.* NA

The workshops of the French arsenal shipyard fitters, which suffered a great deal from allied bombings. U-Boot-Archiv Coll.

Plan of Kéroman III *sent by the French Resistance to London. PRO Coll.*

trains derailed. The French arsenal workers also carried out acts of passive resistance, i.e. by demonstrating during the British aviators' funerals, on 30 December 1940, then three times in 1941, by deserting the streets of Lorient, on 1 January 1941, following the instructions of General De Gaulle over the radio, by 3,000 men parading in front of the war memorial for the Joan of Arc feast day, on 20 May 1941, by more than 6,000 people accompanying the workers designated to be sent to work in Germany to the railway station in October 1942, at which time "*L'Internationale*" was sung and hostile chanting took place: "*A bas les Boches*", "*Laval au poteau*", "*Les Soviets partout*", and also "*A mort Stosskopf*" (*Down with the Krauts, Hang Laval, Soviets everywhere, Death to Stosskopf*).

The emblems of the two U-Boote *fleets present in Lorient, according to the American manual. Coll. NA*

Confidential

SUBMARINE.

A submarine on a cross is the device of the 10th U-boat Flotilla.

Drawn from description by P/W.

SUBMARINE, GRAY, WITH SIEGRUNE

Device of the 2nd U-boat Flotilla based on Lorient.

Drawn from description.

Who was this person that the workers wished to see dead? He was the deputy manager of the arsenal, from Alsace, who passed for the perfect collaborator, when he was, in fact, the leading Resistant of the arsenal, who the base was named after in 1946! Deputy to the Engineer General Antoine, from the start of the Occupation he got in touch with the head of the north sector of the *Deuxième Bureau* (Second Office) (espionage) of the French Navy in Vichy, to which he gave an account of the German work every month, for which he provided plans, and above all, the movements of the *U-Boote*. This information was then sent to the American Embassy.

When unoccupied France was invaded in November 1942, he then turned to the Alliance information network, which took responsibility for passing the information to England. However, the dismantling of this net-

In July 1946, the Kéroman submarine base was officially named after the assistant manager of the French arsenal who gave his life for the Resistance. LB Coll.

work in September 1943 made his task much harder, before he was finally found out. Since he had informed the Allies in the greatest of secrecy, his arrest by the German security services, on 21 February 1944, surprised everyone, except the rare members of staff to have been kept in confidence and who provided him with information, notably an anti-Nazi German engineer posted in Lorient. The engineer, Stosskopf, was shot by the Germans on 1 September 1944, at the Struthof camp in Alsace.

He was not the only officer of the French shipyard to have carried out intelligence. One of the most famous is Alphonse Tanguy, engineer at the arsenal, who entered the Confrérie Notre Dame network organized by Gilbert Renault, better known under the name of "Colonel Rémy". At the end of December 1941, Alphonse Tanguy brought all the plans of the different submarine bases on the Atlantic coast to Paris. He had stolen them directly from a German safe, for which he had a copy of the keys! Following the arrest of the network's radio chief, Alphonse Tanguy was shot in Paris, on 5 November 1943.

Patch of the 8th US Army Air Force.

The allied bombings

The British did not take long to react to the presence of the *U-Boote* in Lorient. During the second half of 1940, they were very active, but with very limited resources. The first British air raid on Lorient, carried out by 12 aircraft, took place on the night of 22 August 1940. After two bombings limited to Lorient early in the month of September, the Bomber Command carried out the first large air raid, on the night of 27 September, with 35 aircraft. This resulted in 32 civilian victims. It was the start of a very long series of bombings. Already, three other attacks were made up to the end of the month. In October, the *RAF* bombed Lorient 12 times, but with limited resources, using 1 to 6 planes each time. The air raids were intensified in November, with 17 bombings which were almost daily, from 7 to 15 and 19 to 23 November, generally carried out with less than 10 planes. The people of Lorient experienced 20 air raids of the same scale in December. To counter these attacks, the German navy, charged with the anti-aircraft defence of the port, continued to be strengthened, reaching the size of a brigade. On 27 December, the German cruiser, *Admiral Hipper*, entered the port of Brest. This new situation brought some respite to Lorient in the following two months, while the attacks were concentrated on Brest.

In January 1941, only three air raids were made on Lorient with roughly five bombers used each time. In February, when the work really began on Kéroman, the British only carried out one air raid with one plane on Port Louis. On 2 February, the Germans set up thirty or so barrage balloons to prevent planes coming too close at low altitude. However, the month of March shows that the British bombing resumed with 4 large air raids between 15 and 22 March, with an overall total of more than 110 aircraft, which were primarily aimed at the arsenal sector. Again, the city of Lorient would benefit from some respite. On 22 March, the *Scharnhorst* and *Gneisenau* cruisers entered the port of Brest where all the British resources were then concentrated. A

On February 7, 1943, US Captain Richard Brock presented a sketch of the Keroman site as a bombing target to student pilots at San Angelo School in Texas. Coll. NA

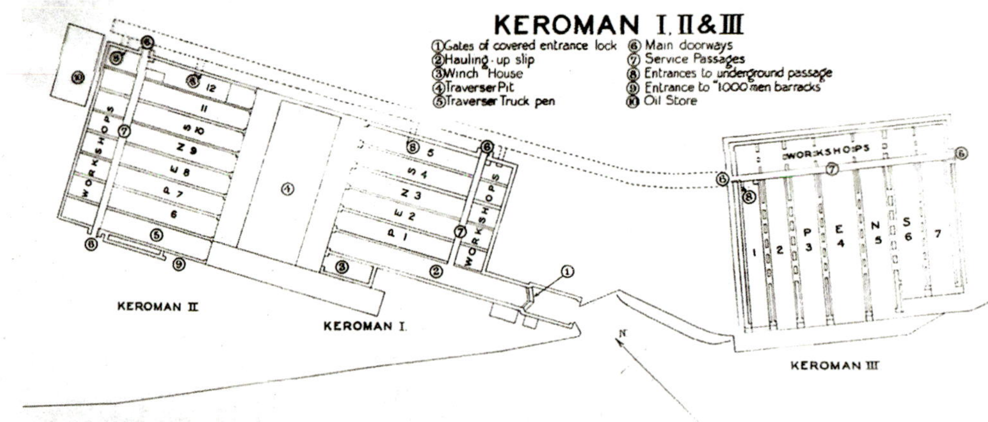

American plan of the three bases of KI, KII *and* KIII. *Coll. NA*

single air raid with 20 bombers was carried out on Lorient in April. In this instance, these were planes which were rerouted from Brest, because of cloud cover! In May, when the work on the *KI* and *KII* bases was at the delicate stage of the formwork, only two air raids, using 10 planes overall, were carried out, and not a single one in June! All the same, in July, 47 planes attacked the arsenal area, but without jeopardizing the base's shipyards just beside it. In August, no air raid was reported and only 4 planes came to Lorient, rerouted from Le Havre, in September 1941, even though the small Scorff base and *Kéroman I* were now operational and covered by a concrete roof resisting the largest British bombs at the time.

Nothing happened either in October. It was not until the night of 23 November that 53 bombers were sent to Lorient. It was already too late! No air raid was made in December, even though *Kéroman II* was brought into service.

In January 1942, a single bomber came to Lorient dropping four explosive bombs and, for the first time, 120 incendiary bombs. On 12 February, the three *Kriegsmarine* ships stationed in Brest, at which all the air attacks were aimed, managed to leave this port and return to Germany. However, no bombing mission was carried out on Lorient in March, only one in April, with 17 bombers, despite the fact that the *Kéroman III* construction site had got into full swing, and none in May, or during the following months. It was not until 21 October 1942, that the bombers appeared again in the Lorient sky. This time it was the Americans, who, unlike the British, who had carried out these missions up until then, came in broad daylight. Out of the 90 bombers planned, due to the weather conditions only 15 were able to drop their bomb loads on the port, escorted for this dangerous daylight mission by 116 fighters!

During the America bombings of 6 March 1943, a total of 65 bombers dropped 162.5 tons of bombs on a city already ruined by the air raids of the previous months. National Archives Coll.

The *USAAF* bombers came back twice in November for the submarine bases' installations; the first with 13 planes, the second with only 11 due to the bad weather. 1942 ended with a much heavier bombardment, on 30 December, with 40 American planes dropping 79.6 tons of heavy bombs on Kéroman, of which the last part, *KIII*, was already virtually completed. The British also carried out hundreds of magnetic mine laying operations in the harbour of Lorient, the result of which was the destruction of three *U-Boote*, between September 1942 and April 1943.

After these hesitant operations, which enabled the Germans to build their bases in Lorient fairly peacefully for two and a half years, 1943 was to be a year of agony for the city and its inhabitants. In England, on 14 January 1943, following the carnage of the merchant ships sunk in the Atlantic by the German submarine force, the British War Cabinet sent a clear directive to Air Marshall Harris, in command of the Bomber Command, nicknamed "Bomber Harris":

"*A decision has been taken to submit the following bases to a maximum scale of attack at night with the object of effectively devastating the whole area in which are located the submarines, their maintenance facilities, and the services, power, water and light, communications, etc. and other resources upon which their operations depend*"

The first of the bases on the following list was Lorient. The same evening, on the night of 14 January 1943, the 317th air raid warning was given in the city. The *RAF* sent 128 bombers, 99 of which carried out the mission by dropping 73.6 tonnes of explosive bombs and 83,548 incendiary bombs, the majority of which fell on the city centre, where more than 80 fires broke out. The British came back the following evening. Out of the 154 planes planned, 132 carried out their mission, dropping 140.4 tons of standard bombs and 87,163 incendiary bombs. The city counted 400 fires. The Americans took over, on 23 January, with 36 B-17 bombers. Around forty buildings were destroyed in the city. However, Lorient's agony was far from over. On the night of 23 January, 100 bombers were sent by the RAF, 47 of which dropped their bombs on the city. Again on the night of 26 January, out of the 168 bombers planned, a total of 136 dropped 80 tons of bombs and 56,687 incendiary bombs. The month of January ended with a 6th massive British bombardment, on the night of 29 January, during which 130 bombers were sent to drop 50.7 tons of bombs.

The month of February 1943 was not any better, with 4 air raids deployed using even greater means of destruction. It started with a first British air raid, on the night of 4 February, carried out by 120 planes out of the 128 planned, in which 90.6 tons of bombs and 63,376 incendiary bombs fell on the port and city. The worst, however, was yet to come. On the night of 7 February, 296 British bombers out of the 352 planned, dropped 254.1 tons of bombs! The civilian population, which had started to evacuate the city around mid-January, for the majority, had already made its exodus. Out of the 46,000 inhabitants registered in 1939, there

The civilian population of Lorient evacuating the city. Here a bus standing in front of the bus station on Cours Chazelles, enables the last residents to leave with what little baggage they had. The large building which had lost its roof, called "Haus Jürst", had been requisitioned for the staff of the 10th Flotilla. After the war, the Café Jules Simon opened there. LB Coll.

The American bombing of 17 May 1943, with 118 planes dropping 289.5 tons of bombs seems to have been one of the most precise in the sector. Several impacts can be noted on the roof of the Kéroman bases, while the workshop area was severely touched by high-calibre bombs. National Archives Coll.

The concrete tower placed beside Kéroman I, *built to be used as a training centre for the evacuation of submerged submarines, was hit by a bomb and damaged. The thicker roof of the bases, however, remains intact.* BA Coll.

only remained about 500 people living among the ruins. The already considerable number of bombers used was increased for the following air raid by the RAF. On the night of 13 February, 422 planes out of the 476 planned dropped in excess of 500 tons of bombs (524.3 tons), with some 26,168 incendiary bombs, 5,000 of which were 7.5 times heavier than those used up to then. Three days later it continued with 360 British bombers dropping 461.9 tons of bombs and, above all, 230,916 incendiary bombs! To reassure the staff working in the bases, the *Generaladmiral* Marschall, high commander of the Navy in the West, noted in his agenda for 16 February 1943:

"*The Lorient Navy arsenal, commanded by Rear Admiral Matthiae, has had to deal with a considerable number of heavy air raids in the last few weeks. The English have not attained their objective, which was to put the submarine base out of action. Even if there has been huge damage to the city and the buildings of the old arsenal, the submarine dry docks will continue relentlessly. Through their dynamism, relentlessness, and pronounced determination not to be discouraged, the command and the troops of Lorient have succeeded in protecting and repairing by far the great majority of the machines and equipment. I would like to express my gratitude to the arsenal commander, to his section leaders and all the staff".*

The city was nothing more than rubble, and yet the air raids continued in the months to follow: American bombing, on 6 March 1943, with 65 planes unloading 162.5 tons of bombs, British bombing on the night of 2 April, with 40 planes out of the 48 planned, dropping 117.1 tons of bombs, American bombing on 16 April, with 56 B-17s dropping 147 tons, and finally, the last American bombing of the year on 17 May 1943, with 118 B-17s and B-24s dropping 289.5 tons of bombs. Unfortunately, these sad figures reflect great hardship for the civilians of Lorient, 206 of whom died, many others remaining disabled and all of whom lost the majority of their property and belongings.

The year 1944 was calmer. The submarine bases continued to operate until the Normandy landings. On 6 August 1944, when the Americans started to liberate Brittany, at 7.50 p.m. in full daylight, 11 British *Lancaster* bombers carried standard bombs and 11 others, each carried the new 5.4 ton bomb, the most powerful ever to be used against Lorient, called the *Tallboy*! Four hits were marked in the sector, one of which was to the roof of *KIII*, to pens *K21-22*, but the damage was minimal. Following the encircling of the city by the American and French troops, these bombing campaigns stopped, because the Germans had evacuated their U-Boote to Norway. After the war the British Chief of Defence, recognized their major strategical error in not having bombed the bases during their construction, when they were really vulnerable.

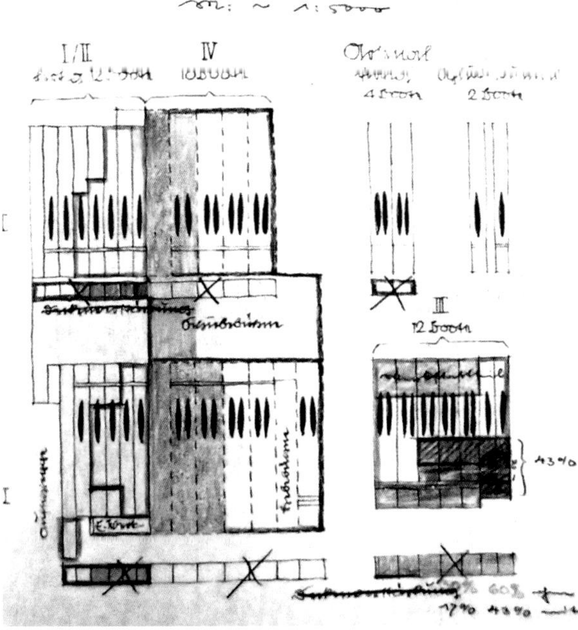

Plan of all the submarine shelters in Lorient planned by the Organization Todt in Lorient: 30 protected places are created for the U-Boote *with* KI, KII, *the Scorff base, the* Dom Bunkers *and* KIII. *The extension of* Keroman IV, *which was to accommodate 18 new Type XXI submarines, will never be completed. Coll. NA*

The uncompleted Kéroman IV *projects for type XXI submarines*

In 1943, the German shipyards implemented a construction development for a new type of revolutionary submarine, which should have been operational by the end of 1944. This was the XXI type.

The Lorient base was the only base established on the French coast, destined to receive them. With this objective, during the summer of 1943, a new gigantic construction site was to begin, parallel to that of *Kéroman I* and *II*, which would prolong the existing system of travelling platforms. Two new bases called *KIVa* and *KIVb*, built ashore, had to be capable of

3-dimensional plan of the full installations planned for Kéroman. In the background the large KIVa *and* KIVb *bases, which were to receive the new type XXI* U-Boote.
Coll HDB Bildarchiv, Berlin

protecting a total of 18 type XXI *U-Boote*! These were too tall to use the existing installations.

Initially, the construction work focussed on the *KIVa* base, built beside *KI*, which had to include 4 dry pens, 1 wet dock and an area protecting the slipway, to bring up the XXI types which would end up on the fishing port. Two new ultra-modern submarines could be housed together in a single pen. These were increased in size, to measure 23 m wide. The completed *KIVa* base was to measure 160 m long by 130 m wide. The roof was planned with a thickness of 7 m, surmounted by the *Fangrost* structure. In December 1943, only the lateral inter-pen walls alongside *KI*, intended for the laying of a railway linking *KIII*, and those of the two first pens, were being completed. Their rear section, intended for the workshops was partially covered by a concrete roof.

The work in progress on *KIVa* was not disturbed by the allied bombings, but it suffered from a lack of materials and labour. It was finally completed on 24 April 1944, leaving priority to the more urgent construction sites of the Atlantic Wall.

The *KIVb* base, smaller in size, 95 m long and 150 m wide, had to include 3 pens, each capable of housing 2 type XXI *U-Boote*. The work

This part of KIVa was built parallel to Kéroman I, of which the left edge can be seen. The space between these two bases was to be covered with concrete to enable material trains to go directly to KIII under cover. LB Coll.

The rear of KIVa *was comprised of repair workshops. LB Coll.*

stopped at digging the foundations and at the start of the formwork for a few of the pen walls.

The base workshops' special constructions during the Lorient Pocket

Six days after the Normandy landings of 6 June 1944, the German shipyards began to evacuate their female staff. A first bus convoy of 80% German women workers left Lorient for Strasbourg. On 12 July, a second convoy carried most of the others to Paris, where they took the train to Germany. There only remained a few dozen telephone and radio operators, and nurses from the Red Cross. The work continued on the shipyard submarines, but spare parts for the assembly of the snorkels could no longer reach them by lorry.

On 1 August 1944, General Patton's American troops broke through the German front in Avranches and, from then on, began to liberate Brittany. Three days later the city of Rennes was already in the hands of the Allied troops. On 3 August, the camps of Hennebont were abandoned and the German workers fell back to Kéroman.

The same day, General Wilhelm Fahrmbacher, commander of the whole army in Brittany, who had left his headquarters in Pontivy the day before, came to find refuge with his staff in Kéroman in the barracks for the 1,000. He took charge of the besieged city. On 5 and 6 August, the minesweepers of the 2nd Flotilla left Lorient, bringing with them several hundred shipyard workers who landed further south to return to Germany. On 6 August, the British bombers dropped their 5.4 ton Tallboy bombs on the bases. On 7 August 1944, the port of Lorient was finally besieged by the American army and the French

Unterschrift d. Inhabers

Inhaber dieses Ausweises, der Kurt Rach

geb. 8. 3. 11. zu Wilhelmshaven

ist gemäss § 7 des Wehrgesetzes zum aktiven Wehrdienst einberufen und ist während dieser Zeit Soldat der deutschen Wehrmacht

Der Ausweis hat nur mit Lichtbild Gültigkeit, ohne Lichtbild nur unter gleichzeitiger Vorlage des Wehrpasses.

Paris, den 26. 7. 44.

Siegel

Pass issued in January 1944 and stamped by the Lorient shipyard, notifying that, from then on, the worker, Rach, was part of the military forces of the Wehrmacht. *On 17 January 1944, the port of Lorient was given the status of Atlantic Wall fortress. LB Coll.*

Early August 1944, the members of the U-Boote's 2nd Flotilla staff ashore were sent ahead of the American army which was coming to liberate central Brittany. UBA Coll.

forces of the Resistance. Inside this Pocket, 27,000 workers and soldiers in German uniforms had sufficient stocks to last for 56 days.

Thanks to retrieving the food depots in Hennebont and Quimperlé, and agricultural requisitions, as well as very strict rationing and imports by boats from the Pocket of St. Nazaire every 3 weeks, they would be able to hold out until May 1945.

The workers who stayed at Kéroman received the order to complete the work on the *U-Boote*, which were evacuated to Norway by 5 September at the latest. The U-155 was the last to leave on that date. On 16 August, a last convoy of boats left the besieged city, taking the last German women staff, leaving only the nurses on site. In the last days of September, the

On 8 November 1944, a small party was organized in Kéroman for the 25th anniversary of an officer of the K.M.W. Lorient. *The clothing was highly varied. On his jacket lapel the worker in civilian clothes (second to the left) is wearing the decoration for meritorious workers of the Shipyards of the West.* LB Coll.

A better than usual meal and champagne were distributed in the Kéroman base to celebrate the New Year in 1945. There was a mixture of civilian workers, soldiers and sailors. The walls were decorated with paintings suggesting being surrounded, the return back home and women. LB Coll.

An arm badge, which would be a siege souvenir for the German soldiers, was made in the base workshops, on the request of the fortress commander, General Fahrmbacher. Made from white iron from tin cans, it represents a naked soldier straddling the submarine base. Ironically, this badge was nicknamed "the naked man from Pontivy" by the German soldiers, following the hasty arrival of the General, in Lorient, from his headquarters in Pontivy, fleeing ahead of the American troops. LB Coll.

German staff of General Fahrmbacher moved into Kernevel, the old submarine headquarters. On 10 September, *Vizeadmiral* Matthiae was named commander of the Naval Defence of Lorient. On 19 September, the German hospital ship, *Rostock*, loaded with 300 seriously injured, left Lorient, to be immediately inspected by the Allied fleet.

Several boats of the 14th Flotilla of submarine chasers, which maintained a regular link with the St. Nazaire Pocket, found shelter in *Kéroman III*, where they were protected from Allied artillery.

They were obliged to remove their main mast in order to enter the pens. Three reserve companies were used on the Pocket front, formed from German shipyard workers having received rapid infantry training. Out of the remaining 1,000 men in Kéroman, 400 were again turned into infantry men in early 1945. Those that remained on site were grouped into 4 new companies, two of which were charged with the destruction of the arsenal and the German installations in the event of an attack by the Allies.

The workers, who received a half-day of infantry training every 15 days, finished setting up a steam energy electrical installation which would be operational in February 1945.

As the Lorient Pocket was completely surrounded, the base workshops were put to work to build the equipment needed for siege war:

- in relation to armaments, carriages were built to make the guns from the anti-aircraft defence batteries, disarmed ships and stocks initially intended for the *U-Boote*, mobile and ready for road use. Shields to protect their gunners and aiming devices were also made. The workers adapted a 12.8 cm anti-aircraft defence gun to a truck to create mobile artillery on rails! They also mounted a 10.5 cm gun on a lorry to make it a motorized gun. An "armoured detachment" was even formed by placing metal sheets and machine guns on two lorries and 7 cars, while an old French Renault tank, which was used to flatten the runways at the airfield was provided with a flamethrower tube. Due to a lack of petrol, this detachment never went into action. Tubes for the *Panzerfaust*, anti-tank guns and rifle grenade launchers were also built.

A souvenir postcard for 1 January 1945 was printed in Lorient. It was sent to St. Nazaire by boat and then to Germany by plane from the Escoublac La Baule airfield! LB Coll.

- For transportation, due to the lack of fuel, vehicles were given equipment to run on a gas generator. Since the Germans had 1,300 horses, horse-drawn carriages were assembled as well as harnessing equipment.

- When it came to health, they made stretchers, prostheses and crutches for the hospitals. In addition, 600 beds were set up in Kéroman, with this objective, in case of an attack by the Allies.

- For the troops' comfort, 500 kitchen utensils left the workshops, as well as 6,000 infantry shovels, gaiters, shoe nails and even wooden clogs! With regard to clothing, hundreds of blue trousers were dyed in green and raincoats were made from the fabric of the old barrage balloons, protection against aerial bombardment. The equipment in the barracks for the 1,000 enabled the besieged Germans to watch films, variety shows, as well as many concerts!

March 1945, the marines confined in Kéroman were called together. Clothing was extremely varied: camouflage caps, woollen and leather jackets. On the right, the uncompleted work of KIVa. *LB Coll.*

Since the large doors protecting the Kéroman II *pens no longer needed to be opened during the siege, barracks to accommodate a few more men were built in front of them, where they were sheltered from American artillery.*
Pascal Theffo Coll.

The French Navy recovers the submarine bases

In Etel, on 8 May 1945, the Commander of the German forces of the Lorient Pocket signed an unconditional surrender. The Allied forces liberated the area two days later, and the French Navy then entered Kéroman, which was handed over intact. In addition to the operation bases, the French Navy recovered two *U-Boote*, only one of which, the U-123, could be repaired.

On 19 May, the French government decided to retain these installations and establish a submarine centre in Lorient. On 31 July, the British submarine, Curie, was the first to come into dry dock. Following the Liberation, the French Navy had 13 pre-war French submarines, 7 submarines lent by the British Navy and 6 *U-Boote* as spoils of war. Five of these were posted in Lorient in April 1946, and from the end of the following year, together with the few French pre-war submarines, made up the "2[e] *Escadrille de sousmarins*" (2nd submarine squadron).

General De Gaulle's visit confirmed the utmost importance of these installations to France. On 6 July 1946, the base was officially named "*Engineer General Stosskopf*" in honour of the former assistant manager of the arsenal, a Resistance fighter shot on 1 September 1944. As for the concrete tower standing beside *KI*, used as a training centre for the rescue of German submariners, rehabilitated by the French Navy in 1953, this was named the "*Davis Tower*" in tribute to the British inventor of the submerged escape device for submarines.

On 10 May 1945, the French Navy recovered the Kéroman installations delivered intact. This photo, in which we can see KI and KII to the left and KIII to the right, was taken from Kernevel. ECPAD

In May 1945, the area around Kéroman was completely destroyed, only the bunkers stood up to the bombardments. SHM Coll.

On 14 September 1955, the French submarine, Andromède, *of the Aurore type, left* Kéroman II *on its cradle to be launched again.* DR

These two signs, found in 2007 on the 2nd floor of the workshops above the slipway winch mechanism, were used to categorize spare parts for the type VII U-Boote, *by the French Navy.* LB Coll.

From the beginning of the 1950s, the French arsenals built new Diesel-electric submarines, which replaced the pre-war and wartime models. Operational from 1957 to 1960, 6 ocean-going *Narval* type submarines, directly inspired by the German XXI type, were posted in Lorient. The last of these was withdrawn from active service in 1993. One of them, the *Espadon*, can now be visited in St. Nazaire. From 1964 to 1970, smaller and more easily manoeuvrable fighting submarines were brought into service. These were *Daphné* type submarines. Of the 11 built, 8 were posted in Lorient.

The Daphné *type,* Flore *submarine, declared unfit for service by the Navy in 1989, was left in Kéroman. Converted into a museum in 2010, it stands on the esplanade between* KI *and* KII. LB Coll.

The last was declared unfit for service in 1998. One of them, the *Flore*, declared unfit for service in 1989, was left by the Navy at Kéroman and was converted into a museum in 2010. The last class of conventional submarines posted to Lorient was the high-performing Agosta type. 4 of them; brought into service between 1977 and 1978, served in the "Atlantic Submarine Squadron", the new name of the Lorient flotilla, since 1970.

These conventional Diesel-Electric attack submarines were doomed to disappear with the choice of building nuclear-powered device-launching submarines made in the 1960s. The Lorient squadron was finally disbanded in June 1995. The *Daphné* type *Sirène* submarine was the last to leave the base in February 1997. The slipway mechanism was still in working condition at the time!

End of the 1990s. This French submarine, waiting in front of the fishing port slipway, was soon to be scrapped. It is the symbol of the end of 50 years of French Navy presence in Kéroman. Michel Quettier Coll.

The old military zone now looks to the world of sailing, and the Kéroman I *and* II *installations are surrounded by boat sheds in which multihulls are prepared for racing. To the left we can see the large building of the Cité de la Voile Eric Tabarly, inaugurated on 17 and 18 May 2008.* LB Coll.

Kéroman on July 6, 1946, the base was officially named "Underwater Base Engineer General Stosskopf", in tribute to the former director of the arsenal assassinated by the Germans on the night of September 1 to 2, 1944. When this plaque will be replaced many years later by another in metal, the base will have been renamed "General Engineer Stosskopf submarine base", due to the new name of the Lorient flotilla in 1970: "the Submarine Squadron of Atlantic". Coll. ECPAD

Conclusion

Today, after many years and a variety of projects, the Kéroman site, which was returned to the city of Lorient, is redirected towards the world of sailing. The space inside the bases ashore has been completely renovated. *KI* houses Catlantech and Lorima, yacht makers, while *KII* is being used again by the deck hardware company, Plastimo. Three large modern boat sheds have been built around these two bases for the preparation of multihulls for racing. The Cité de la Voile Eric Tabarly, in a huge 18,000 m² construction built close by, was opened in April 2008.

In terms of heritage, visitors can visit the *Flore* submarine placed on the esplanade between *KI* and *KII*. The Lorient Tourist Office also organizes guided tours of the *KIII* base to tell its story: more than 25,000 visitors flock each year to see and try to understand how this colossal construction works. The "Château des Sardines" in Kernevel, the former residence of Admiral Doenitz, used since the end of the conflict by the French Admiral, commander of the maritime district, is visited every year during heritage days. Finally, the small base of Scorff, located in the town of Lanester, is currently abandoned.

The interior of the 19-20a-20 pen today... Coll. LB